Tylerbody was complete.
It did not know that it was. (But then no
  part of it had ever really understood
  completeness.)
Nor did it know what it was. (How could it?
  It had never existed before.)

But somehow it now had to come to a consciousness
  of being, an awareness of what it was. It might
  tear itself apart and die many deaths in the
  process. But learn it must. Because in
  the multi-faceted uncertainties of its world
  one particular terror was certain. To remain
  static was babbling idiocy.

Yet the world—and this it could not know—might
  not survive the maturing of Tylerbody.

STARMIND

Dave Van Arnam

BALLANTINE BOOKS · NEW YORK

To
Ted and Robin White
who help

CHAPTER ONE

BENJY TYLER stood up and stretched, then dropped to pushup position, hands and toes on the floor. At nineteen his six-foot body, stripped to trunks, showed its sleek strength as it glistened with the exertion of his exercises.

Pushups made his breath increase its slow pace slowly, until at the count of fifty his body's messages told him to stop.

Slowly he rose to his feet and flexed muscles again. The pungent aroma of sweat and the sour staleness of gym equipment was clear in his nostrils. He looked about him absently, seeking inspiration for another exertion before the buzzer could sound.

But the signal came before the inspiration.

Benjy jumped at the sound, then looked about him, now frantically desperate for some alternative.

The buzzer jolted into him again.

He knew it meant it was time for the other room, with the water—the water that stung in his eyes and mouth and nose.

He didn't like the water room.

He sat down in the middle of the exercise room and burst into tears.

A door to the exercise room opened, and Benjy heard a familiar harsh, impatient voice.

"Come on, dummy, get off your behind and stop bawling. There's the antiseptic shower and then the rubdown. You know you like the rubdown, so come on, will you?" Today the voice was more bored than impatient—almost wheedling, Benjy recognized, though "impatient" and "wheedling" were words far beyond his vocabulary.

But there were some words he knew: "dummy," that was one of them, "dummy," that was a bad word. It made his mother cry, and it used to make his father wince so that Benjy wanted to cry, back when his father was still at home. As his limited mind was purely pragmatic, he had never wondered since about his father. But he had known from then on that "dead" was another bad word.

He knew "rubdown" too, and he liked the sensations of the massage. He liked to notice each muscle tensing and relaxing in perfect harmony with the tough hands pummeling his back.

Once more placid, occupied with the most recent concept presented him, he rose and followed the attendant, and suffered the stinging shower that gave him his morning dose of antibiotics that would work their way into his skin a short distance and form a first line of defense against diseases attacking from the outside. By 2053, almost three-quarters of a century had passed since the India-China plaguewars had taken the lives of more than half the world's population, but the antiseptic showers remained.

The attendant whistled tunelessly as he worked the controls modifying the force and temperature of the treated water, and once more Benjy observed the attendant's face and tried to purse his lips the same way. Since, as usual, he did not blow any air through his lips, the result was simply once more to puzzle the attendant. Originally he'd thought the dummy was actually trying to imitate his whistle; but even he could not believe Benjy was so slow-witted as not even to know how to whistle.

So it remained a mystery for both of them.

From the shower Benjy went naked to the next station unbidden. This was the steam room; while he was there it was kept only warm, not steaming. Benjy had early indicated that steam completely terrified him— the first time in it, he screamed with animal anguish and battered his way entirely through the wooden door when the hot white billows had started pouring into the steam room.

The attendant didn't have to ask Benjy to get onto the table; up he went, and stretched out on the resilient, absorbent material. The attendant stepped up beside the table and began slapping and battering at the strong back.

Exercise, eating, and more exercising had been Benjy's life at the sanitarium, and his future was only more of the same. Of all the toys and games and attempts at education, the one thing that had gotten through Benjy's too-few cerebral interconnections was that exercise was both fun and worthwhile. Nothing else from that time on held any interest for him.

Benjy would have been rich, had he been competent to receive his father's fortune.

Jailyn Rost was indisputably rich, and she had made a point of being competent.

A murmur of surprise wafted among the passengers of the spaceship *Miles High* as the lights slowly dimmed, then went off leaving only the palely glowing green of the translucent, gently phosphorescent wall panels.

The *Miles High* was dipping through the rings of Saturn, and the sleet of rocks glittered with all colors in the dense, cold, reflected light of the giant planet.

A devil dance of eerie hues dappled the wall-high

viewscreen. Jostling rocks skimmed near the ship, floating first in the distance and then fleeting by them as
the thirty-three passengers caught their breath in
wonder.

Venusian cave incense filled the entire viewscreen
cabin, adding to the silent dreamlike beauty.

"Mmmm," said Parker, cocking his head at the
lovely, dark-haired girl. "Most impressive. With a solar
system full of sights like this . . . well, to be rich and
to be able to go where one wants . . ." He grinned
helplessly and shrugged his shoulders. "I suppose that
when you're born to it, though, it doesn't seem the
same as it does to a poor middle-class glorified reporter
like me."

Jailyn Rost studied the slight, wiry figure beside her.
"I assumed when you contacted me on Saturn Station
about this *fascinating* full-length feature study you
want to do about me, that you had bothered to do some
preliminary studying. Surely whoever financed you to
the rings must have required—"

Parker smiled. "*Interlife* made sure I know a very
great deal about your activities, Miss Rost. But I know
almost nothing of your personality—except of course
that I now know you jump to conclusions. Yes, yes,"
he went on over her attempted interruption, "I know
the *Miles High* is packed with testing and recording
instruments. I know you spend more time checking over
equipment than you do escorting a bunch of rich-bitch
ne'er-do-wells from pleasure spot to pleasure spot. I
know that, rich as you are, you couldn't possibly afford
this ship without special arrangements with Transfed
about all the information this ship keeps generating,
and I know a lot about those arrangements that I won't
even bother hinting about."

He hesitated and glanced meaningfully around the
room at the scattered clusters of gapers staring at the
rings, then went on without a real pause. "For that
matter, I know when you took your first space trip,

your first lover, and your last drink. *Now* I am to find out what this adds up to."

"What it adds up to?" She laughed, and concealed her curiosity as to whether he really *did* know of her first lover. A deep breath from an eddy of the pungent Venusian incense momentarily called back a vision of her first glimpse of one of the magic caves, richly glittering with the semicrystallized vegetable deposits used in the incense. The precious stuff was also a mild mind drug, of course; and you could get too much of it if you were very careless, and see things you didn't like. But since the Time of the Changes people didn't mind that so much—though everyone knew that too much of it, and you'd go staggering off to the country to rot.

Parker studied her while telling himself he wasn't; someone as vibrant and lovely as that, you didn't study the techniques. If you were human you relaxed and breathed the cave-mist fumes and let her zap.

Wasn't just human, Parker told himself, then recognized his bemusement. *Am not. Reporter. Very important.* He rather regretted the presence of the cave-mist fumes.

She smiled at him again, and just in time he realized that she had not read his thoughts; what had he been about to say. . . ?

"Have you seen my rusty palace on the Upper Middle Grand Çanal?" She tossed her dark brown curls in unexpectedly girlish joy, and started to tell him of her latest project.

A touch of warmth glowed inside him. He looked about him absently at the other passengers as he followed her words, seeing the gleaming metal walls, the thin clouds of incense, the stupendous vision of Saturn and his mighty rings, and he found himself formulating phrases that would announce to her he hadn't wanted to bother to come all the way out here. Dammit, it wasn't necessary to toss away confederate funds;

after what had happened ten years ago, there were certain debts that had to be paid, after all; far more important.

He caught himself too late, realizing that his left hand had already risen to his waist and had turned itself palm outward—Paulsted's customary gesture.

"Damn the man," he muttered, realizing, again too late, that he was speaking aloud and that he had not been listening to her for some time. Quietly frantic, he tried to recall her words . . . trip back to Mars now . . . building the palace . . . ok, he already knew about that. . . .

"Paulsted," she said, sympathetically waving away the obvious fact that he had not been paying attention to her. "You can't possibly have any liking or respect for him, can you? Especially after your piece on him." It was time to give him the fact that he too had been researched. "But Paulsted sets his myths in strongly, doesn't he?"

Her lips settled into an expression he first, paranoically, took for a sneer at him. *Too easy*, he told himself immediately thereafter, then wished once more that the cave incense would drift away so that he could clear his nose, his eyes, his mind. *She doesn't like Paulsted either, of course*, secondary analysis was telling him simultaneously.

"You're smirking now," she said, and was there a sharp tone? Or—"You're as close as you need to be, actually," the cool sweet feminine tones came. His ears accepted it and his nerves kicked in with a jolt that staggered him. *Overload? Probably not. But there was something wrong in her words, or was there? Damn this life of nuances!*

"He isn't a dictator, though," he found himself saying, prodding at her with old habit, and he wanted to laugh at the way he continued to function as a reporter even when the fumes made him want to go to sleep.

"Of course," she said. She laughed. "Is it part of your charade, then?" she asked, not unpleasantly. "Setting me up for political statements your researches haven't satisfied you about? You did it well—an 'involuntary' gesture to remind me . . .'"

"Oh, well, the gesture was involuntary enough," he said, abandoning games for the time being. "You didn't expect me to pass up the chance, did you?"

"Of course not; that's why you're good at your job. But you might as well know that I don't really think of Paulsted as a blackhat. Oh, yes, I don't like him detouring funds from my favorite space-exploration projects. No, I don't think it's worth putting that money into the multiwave researches. That's why I supported the confederation, but it was a last-ditch effort and I knew it was. Paulsted's not dictating to his beloved Transfederal Parliament of Earth and the Colonies, but he's a rabble-rouser, and he finally got the rabble more roused by the multiwave than by dull old space travel that's been around for ninety years and more. But that's the way it is. And I'm still sticking with space travel; there's enough out here to keep the whole race busy for a long time. If Paulsted makes it take a little while longer than a long time, it won't kill us. . . ."

"Yes, of course," Parker agreed calmly. "But the multiwave's such a waste. Potential faster-than-light drives are a worse breed of myth than any other I know of. We've got our future ahead tending to our own solar gardens."

"I don't like him just the same," she admitted frankly, after a pause, "though I don't know why I should tell you. Would I buy a used spaceship from him?" Her lips quirked; Parker smiled thinly.

There was a subdued hiss in the room.

A moment later, over the Alert hiss, came a voice. "Cap'n Rost, the computers are just chuckling away at themselves chewing over all that nice new data we've been feeding in, and I think they're about full-up for a while. Ready for a nice long wasteful trip back to Mars and El Rancho Sandy?"

"I'll fire you yet, you Nauruvian phony," she said with a smile, pressing a wallcom button. "Yes, of course," she added. "Full speed ahead and all that, and over and out, and so forth."

"Over and out, Missy Rost, ma'am, Rusty, sir!"

"I *would* fire him too," she said, lips quirking again; but she had released the wallcom button before speaking. "As it happens, though, he's got a half interest in the computers. *You* know."

"No, as a matter of fact, I don't, Miss Rost." Parker wondered whether she was still bemusing him, or if he was simply about ready to fall completely asleep as he sat there. He began to wish intensely that mind drugs had been made illegal again, after all, in that half-assed reform movement thirty years ago.

"Ancestry, Mr. Parker. Jimmy Tungo's from Nauru. Don't you remember the Io Stock affair back in forty-one?"

"Of course. Oh, I've lost a bundle in satellite stocks, I have, I have," he said ruefully, always willing to talk about his one great unfulfilled dream. "Wish I'd kept up with it long enough to sink a few solits into Io, though. Was Tungo a big holder?"

"Not exactly. Nauru was, actually, though there was never a big publicity thing about it."

"Why should I pretend? Frankly, you've lost me!"

"Nauru. South Pacific island. Flowers, joy, fruit on the trees, you know, and something of a forerunner of contemporary sex mores, such as they are. And a few taboos they finally shucked.

"Nauru was big on phosphates in the last century —whole island, so far as I know, was just one big pile of phosphates. Well, they sold the phosphates eventually right down to the original coral bottom. They made millions over the years, but they used their heads about it. They took a trifle of the money to replace the phosphates with fresh imported soil; that was back just after the Changes. Every man, woman, and duck on the island was worth about, oh, 20,000 oldbucks by the time they'd sold off all their phosphates, and rebuilt the island. Well, by the time the oldbuck had been one-for-one'd with the solit forty years ago, they were worth about a hundred thousand apiece—I guess there were only about 5,000 of them to start with, after the plaguewars—and had twice the living standard of any other place on Earth, just on part of the interest!

"They followed space travel pretty well, and picked up a lot after the solit loosened up interplanetary credit, and I'm sure they said many prayers over the years to the plasma-ion drive. End of it was they got about 85 percent of Io, in one name and another, and, well . . . do you know the latest estimates on what that gunk they found there is gonna be worth, now that they've found what it can do for hydroponics?

"No? Well, I'll introduce you to one of the 10,000 richest people in the world—Jimmy Tungo of Nauru. Owner of a 50 percent interest in the entire computer-bank system of the *Miles High*. Also the best man I've found yet to supervise 'em; I only wish I knew a third of what he does. Of course, Transfed'll probably take him away for the Pluto business, but . . ."

"Um," said Parker. "You suppose Nauru'd like me to write a book about them?" He grinned.

"*If* they thought you were serious, and competent, they'd probably commission you to write it and then see to it there were only 10,000 copies printed. Guess what Emerged Nation would end up with every copy. If that sort of thing appeals to you, why, go ahead!"

"Um," Parker said again, and observed the viewscreen, where Saturn's rings were shifting about; course change for Mars had begun. And Jailyn Rost, eyes dancing, waited once more for his next attempt at understanding her.

"Rock 770, how do I love thee? Let me count the ways."

Joe Winslow whistled a few bars of "Don't Give Me Those Carnation Blues," and looked askance at the dull iron side of the huge multiwave generator. It formed one wall of Winslow's main living and working chamber, and occupied about one-fourth the volume of Asteroid 770.

"Lessee," he said, idly glancing over the banks of controls in front of him, and ticking his fingers off as if counting. "None, I guess. Well, then, I'll rephrase: how do I like thee?"

A slash of holiday lights brightened up the control panel directly in front of him. He touched glowing buttons in appropriate patterns, as the readout screen told him of his progress in bringing the multiwave resonances back to the standby harmonic. There were several dozen multiwave generators installed in asteroids now, in this twelfth year since the first successful one had been shifted to its cross-ecliptic orbit. Right now they were making tests on the latest of these, leaving Winslow with little to do.

He touched other panels, seeking to adjust to the harmonic, until the readout told him he'd have to crawl inside the generator to the focal point. There he could make those seat-of-the-pants adjustments that would satisfy his aroused awareness of the harmonic shift. Humans weren't supposed to be able to perceive the multiwave directly, but any technician who'd ridden with one for more than three years would insist *he* could tell when it was malfunctioning.

But it meant work, when he hadn't expected it. "Sure, sure," he muttered, suddenly exasperated, and kicked the side of the floaterchair he sat in. The electric motor rrrrred up into audible spectra, and the chair quivered.

He worked its controls with his left hand, his lips pursing with anger as the clumsy mechanical gears refused, for the nth time, to engage properly the first time. But presently the chair swiveled around and, with a low whine, moved at a sedate five kph toward the silent bulk of the multiwave generator.

He turned off the motor as he neared the wall, and the chair slowed to a halt. Then he pushed lightly, arms and elbows, against its arms.

Slowly he rose into the air, hovered there for a moment, then began to fall back slowly in the .2g gravity.

Satisfied he wasn't going to get dizzy again, he pushed himself forward toward a manhole-sized opening in the generator side, at chest height.

Propelling himself into the opening and then along the twisting tunnel of nonconducting open mesh, with swimlike motions of his hands barely touching the mesh to move him along, he almost allowed himself to forget the useless weight—"Mass, dammit," he said aloud to himself—of his legs. He had barely the strength to straighten them out even in the almost nonexistent gravity. He could look forward to living with that for the next month or so at least.

He reached the central chamber, the focal point wherein the pseudogravitic multiwave was generated. Powerful though the generator was—the first-level ion drive that made the asteroid maneuverable had perhaps one-fourth its drain on the hydrogen-fusion power core —on standby the multiwave it produced was nowhere near the magnitude that could harm a man. For several minutes, then, Winslow jiggered manual controls between the vision plates installed at a number of points in the ceiling-walls of the central chamber, content in the certainty that he was achieving a precision in the harmonics that the computer was incapable of either detecting or handling. He barely noticed the view on the plates—of the stars on all sides of his asteroid—as he labored to satisfy his arcane urge; and then after a time it was done.

"So long, Monstro," he said aloud, and patted one

"wall" of the spherical chamber. How convenient, he thought, that his job could be done under near-zero-g conditions. It made having to nurse a broken back through four months of its immobilization after microsurgery almost bearable. Reknit by the microsurgeon with cellular-level precision, the once-severed spinal cord would take that long to get used to being itself again.

Winslow was only too aware that had he been born when his father was—1997—he probably would have been stuck with a broken back for the rest of his life. Even with the growth of microsurgery in the late thirties, he would have been in his forties before such an operation as the one three months ago could have been performed—which would have been too old even for the present state of the art. Had Winslow been much older than his twenty-eight years—the same age as his father when Joe had been born, he thought, not for the first time that year—no microsurgeon would have attempted the job. Traumatic shock to the nerve tissue became too large a factor.

He'd thought about his father's chances with a broken back, then dismissed it with the thought that in a day when they'd been successfully transplanting human brains from one body to another for over half a decade it was foolish to be morbid about broken backs. Why, there used to be countless thousands of diseases to die of. With only a handful of mutated nasties left over from the plaguewars, it hardly made much sense to spend time brooding.

"If you want something that has a right to bother a body," he said aloud, as he made the last turn in the tunnel, "this damn imitation birth canal would be a good thing to start off with. Why," he said, immediately breaking away from the previous thought, "why have I taken to talking to myself the last week? Am I getting potty? Gotta be careful . . ."

He stopped talking as he reentered his living quarters and Monstro's control room. Familiar and more comforting things now surrounded him. Banks of controls, a wall of technical manuals . . . containing a very great deal about the very little that was known for certain about the multiwave . . . for a moment the thought came that he lived in a kind of antiseptic shrine celebrating, as did all shrines, an impenetrable mystery.

Looking at the shelves of manuals, he debated playing his Game again, but decided immediately against it. It had been fun trying to list in his head all the possible theories explaining the multiwave, but he'd become quite discouraged halfway into the metaphysical, with the idea that the multiwave was God's simultaneous pronunciation of all his infinite names. That went too far past even the most amusing scientific speculations; his favorite of these being that the multiwave was to be understood as an analogy of the West's sixty-cycle AC hum, considered in terms of that hypothetical universe whose atoms were to be supposed to be the solar systems of this one. It was so elegantly impossible . . .

No, incomplete and occasionally even contradictory as it was, the Pseudogravitic Field Theory contained more truth than any other. The development of the multiwave effect from Shaw's 1988 General Theory of Gravitation was enough, even though Shaw himself had said "Call it serendipity," so convinced was he that the multiwave had nothing whatsoever to do with his beloved theory.

Joe Winslow shrugged off speculation and leaned forward to flick on his threedee, opting for the least tiring recreation.

His left hand paused for a moment, then held stiffly away from his body while he pondered the feeling that had just come over him.

Wrong.

Something wrong . . . somewhere. In spite of all his fiddling and tinkering.

The mechanic's instinct was strong in him, which was why, after all, he was a successful technician shepherding Monstro for good pay through its metaphysical loop-the-loops, and he wondered if something was wrong with the stabilizers, operating off the ion drive.

No, the slightest imbalance there would have alarms flashing all over the room. Probably it was the fact that he knew the threedee was a little out of whack. He shrugged again and wished the supply ship, nicknamed the *Navel*, would come round again with the parts he'd ordered.

The threedee now on, his chair swung round to the controls of the computer, and he checked to see everything was in order. Then his chair swung round once more and he looked at the empty space in front of his reference library.

One more hint of danger roused his instincts again briefly as the threedee image slowly grew; then he made himself relax. "Degenerating circuits?" he said aloud absently, unaware that he had spoken. He refused to worry. The supply ship would be arriving in a few hundred hours or so. Nothing was wrong that couldn't wait.

The threedee solidified . . .

Cloud plume spewing from the peak in a silent banner of vapor, Everest in a brief glimpse shattered into the room, followed by the awesome effect of sliding down its vast mountainside into an ice-choked valley.

Into the valley—and straight down at the North Col, the glacier that creaked and groaned in massive retard past the hugeness of Earth's tallest mountain.

Winslow sighed with recognition and contentment as the view momentarily made it seem he was actually smashing into the glacier itself—and then passed through into the cavern complex underneath.

Foot-high letters of fire formed in a semicircle in front of him as he sat: "The Skycycle Gang Under the Roof of the World."

Cast and credits of the juvenile thriller rolled by in varicolored flames, superimposed on roving views of the caverns. Music thundered up from the background, booming up from subsonics into jagged chords that peaked into sharp drumtaps at the flame-on of each name.

The scene focused onto the mouth of a dark tunnel; then into it he seemed to go, along with the threedee.

Blackness—and he cursed at Monstro's maintenance lights; the computer refused to turn them off and always ruined darkness effects. "I'll get at that program core one of these goddamned days, see if I don't," he muttered. Then he shut up.

He knew what was going to happen in the show, having seen it twenty times and more. And yet he hated the Skycycle Gang threedees, except for this one. This one had . . .

Almost blackness; complete silence. The computer didn't object to temporarily turning off Monstro's white noise, as long as it didn't go on that way too long. White noise was necessary; otherwise, the silence of the cryonics era in space life had a nasty side effect on humans. It could be summed up, he knew, as a kind of instant insanity, except of course that it always took *some* time to have its effect. Before white noise was S.O.P., at least. He approved of the computer's laxity during his threedees. *Some* programer was aware that madness lurked around more than one imaginary corner in space. . . .

Savoring the paradox, he relaxed even further, preparing for that which was to come.

There was a faint glow in the distance—not the

maintenance lights—and the end of the tunnel approached. Beyond lay . . .

The tunnel mouth dissolved into a throne room all glittering with mica-gold, and then a woman's face became all that there was in the universe.

A small chaste set of fiery letters dotted needlessly underneath the matchlessly beautiful face: "Doriada Jinar—"

He closed his eyes for the briefest of moments. The taste of loneliness and the sight of *her* again ached inside him, countering deep in his mind with thoughts of the ten million others, transfixed as he with this girl's incredible beauty. It did not leave him contented, but he was content to wait, if he could but watch her.

At least until the *Navel* came to pick him up for more leave, not that he was good for much until his back finished doing whatever it was doing.

CHAPTER TWO

THE CASTLE reared above the desert sands like a blood-red myth, towered and crenelated as if war among the legendary Sarkush tribes, the long-dead natives of Mars, were ready to break out that afternoon against the terrestrial invaders of the Sacred Land.

Les Parker paused before the heavy iron gate and looked upward at the oxide-rich stones that formed the walls. "Archeologists are going to have fun with that, a few million years from now. . . ."

Jailyn laughed. "That was one of the ideas. Come on, I'll give you the tour!"

She touched her hand to the gate. The patch of chameleon plastic recognized her prints and the gate swung ponderously open, creaking as if strained with the distorting weight of a million years.

They entered side by side, and Parker stopped, waiting for a walkslide.

Jailyn laughed again. "Not here," she said. "We really rough it."

"Fooling archeologists again?"

She thought a moment. "No, I hadn't thought about that, really. I mean, I used chameleon plastic all over the place, the way we do on Earth. I'm not against convenience. And then, there's all the rooms—but let's take things as they come."

Parker walked beside her down the long hallway inside the castle to a great flight of stairs that swooped upward in a daring unsupported curve to the second level.

Beside them as they walked, ranked on either side, stood effigies of men, armored in the ancient styles of Earth. Crude leather bossed with metal studs; awkward early steel plates; then the highly worked suits of the High Middle Ages, almost impossible in combat, yet beautiful to behold if one did not mind that they were stylistic absurdities.

They walked up the curving flight of stairs—and Parker blinked to see the blood-red armor of a Sarkush emperor standing monumentally at the head of the steps, hidden from view from the ground floor and its collection of comparatively crude and recent metalwork.

Ten feet tall the armor stood, with no pretense at the blasphemy of representing inside it the Sarkush ruler who once had worn this priceless symbol of his rank.

Jailyn watched Parker as he walked around the ancient metal. "A recent acquisition?" he asked finally, his eyes still fixed on the splendor of the massive structure.

"No," she said, "a tribute from Mars Commission for my modifications on the mass detector that enabled them to locate Shustan, the capital of the Second Federation. It is what it is, a thing in itself that I love. I do not choose to speak of it in the world, lest I seem too proud of my possessions. It would be dishonorable to *him*." She gestured at the empty armor. "I will ask you not to mention it in what you may choose to write."

He nodded, then shook himself instinctively and turned away from the million-year-old shell.

"Come," Jailyn said, touching him on the forearm and indicating a door behind the pedestal. "My work in progress . . ."

The room was darkened, occupied by cushions in the center which she indicated he should sit among. He did so, and the room sprang into light—

—dim light from a distant star, enriched by curious luminescences on great sky-high crags that towered above him; a chill passed through him or over him and he could not say if the cold was real or only in his soul, touched with the superstitions of a stranger in a land too alien to comprehend.

"Pluto," Jailyn said quietly. "My own recordings. I have reasonably complete tapes of all the interesting and relevant aspects. When I'm finished, it will be like a library of the ten worlds."

"For your private delight?" he prodded gently, knowing they both knew he was prodding.

"In a sense," she said. "It's for poets, actually."

He blinked. "Trumped!"

She walked toward an icy hillock. "Come along," she said. "Have you ever seen the rings from Saturn's surface?"

He rose and followed through the tridee ice heap, which returned to nonexistence at a wave of Jailyn's hand.

Again the next room was dark; this time light sprang up only in the distance—great curved bands of light that resolved themselves after a moment into the familiar swirling rocks of the mighty rings of Saturn, but incalculably richer in color, their light filtered through the alien air above the gas giant's surface.

"Some compensation was necessary here," Jailyn observed, "for the filtering out of much of the light energy. So I'm not entirely satisfied." Then she let Parker absorb the scene.

"Poets," she said after a time—and her voice had become a little pedantic, he thought, as if delivering a speech she'd given before—"always know little of the future. I think. At any rate, there has not been a great age of poetry since the first of the three Elizabeths, and even Shakespeare ignored the New World completely, though it had been discovered more than a hundred years before *Hamlet*.

"It's the same today, sadly; though we've been on the paths of space almost a century and visited every planet in our system, who has captured the meaning in all of it? Few have even tried.

"Oh, glorious fictions have been created, I daresay —adventure writers who perhaps understood more than a thousand starving poets and authors in cold attics. But, as always, the definition of our present remains for the future.

"Well, the future is upon us; space has been ours and yet we still haven't heard what it really means. *That* is why I am constructing this castle with its records of what has been done—and I know how unlikely it is that even this will accomplish anything . . .

"But let me show you the rest."

In silence then they passed through rooms and rooms all filled with planets, now caught in the Red Spot of Jupiter, looking upward with microwaves to the delicate circling satellites; now drifting on wafting dream pods through Venus' poisoned atmosphere, watching the black growths mushroom up and die, yielding to new growths in minutes. . . .

"You don't have Earth," Parker said at last. "Is that on purpose?"

"No," she said. "But I am not a poet; my mind is too active with practicalities. Earth . . . Earth must wait. For someone else. It will take a poet—and much much more."

"Well, then," Parker began, then realized he had nothing to say.

"That's what the rest of this place is for," she said, seeing he had not understood. "To prepare . . . someone . . . so that, some day, he may construct the room for Earth. . . ."

Parker nodded, not fully understanding but unwilling to admit this to the vibrant woman beside him.

"Earth is a place of mountains and rivers and oceans, just like these others," she said, for she saw that again he had not understood. "But Earth has life, and that is part of Earth too. You can't get it all in a scout satellite in three weeks. Oh, I've got some nice scenic shots, but they don't *mean* anything. Not the way they do for the rest of the planets."

"Oh," he said. "Maybe I've got it now." He grinned wryly. "You needn't look hopefully at me; it's obvious I'm no poet!"

She smiled her secret smile; before she could speak, there was a hiss from Jailyn's beltpurse. She touched a stud, and a voice replaced the hiss.

"Miss Rost, this is Stevens, acting for Tungo. The central imploder is acting up again. With Mr. Tungo off at Clarke talking with those Pluto people . . . would you want to come up and take a look?"

"Damn. Off on the other side of Mars when he should—never mind, I'll come up. Send a scooter for me, ok?"

She turned to Parker. "Shouldn't take more than a few hours. The imploder's got a bunch of modifications on it that Jimmy Tungo's worked out, and it's still a bit of a jury-rig. Milt is a good man, but he knows this is a little more than he can handle.

"Still," she went on, a worry line showing on her forehead, "I could wish Jimmy were here too. I wonder if I should wait till he gets—nonsense. My apologies, Mr. Parker; we were just getting started. I've got to get out to the landing pad. With the *Miles High* synching above here, its scooter should be down in a few minutes. You will forgive me?"

Parker shook his head with a smile. "Miss Rost, no man could forgive you for leaving him, least of all myself! But if you're only going to be gone for a few hours . . ."

She *was* nice to be around, he realized. Nicer than it was smart for him to care about. A pretty face and a nice packaging job with the body—but that mind! *We won't even mention all that money,* he said to himself.

. . . Two hours later, the face and the body were burned away, along with most of the drive section of the *Miles High*. The ship glowed for several minutes like a gigantic firefly that couldn't put its tail out.

Her body was burned away like a used match; her head, protected by a heavy beam from the explosion's direct blast, was only ruined on one side.

When Stevens got there, thirty seconds later, with the freezebox, it was only long training that motivated him even to try to nudge the hideous remains into the box with his spacesuited hands.

But because he did, the brain remained alive.

Part of it, at least . . .

Coincidence is not fair, but it *is* impartial. The story of the beautiful woman with everything in life before her, and her death—her virtual death, though the left lobe of her cerebrum had been saved and was being kept alive by the microsurgeons at New Bellevue—spread quickly in space, and Joe Winslow was properly impressed with the tragedy.

"Must have been quite a woman. Worst of it is," he said, aloud, not even caring any more that he was talking aloud, "the grounders'll never bother to think of her."

Two and a half minutes later he decided to do something about what he had supposed were degenerating circuits; they had been bothering him for days with disharmony, and he didn't care that the *Navel* was almost due.

Three minutes later he was suited up and outside Monstro, advancing toward the outer casings of the multiwave generator.

The immense outer horn of the transmitter/receiver loomed above him; whorled much like an ear, it was festooned with countless tiny wires leading away from the outer surface, wires carrying the directives for particular resonances during experiments.

"That's odd—more than odd," he said. Toward the base of the ear, controlling less-used higher resonances, there was a patch of blackened metal, and the fused shards of a number of the threadlike wires.

Energizing a finger of his suit to operate at precision level, he reached for the patch of blackened metal.

The earhorn began splitting open.

There was no time for him to hit the suit's freezebox control, but there was no need to; the suit's encephalographic readings of his brain and body activity sensed the first sharp jagged peak that indicated a total-emergency situation, and as the full force of the transmitter explosion blasted into his body, the multiwave ear shearing away and careening off into space, the freezebox mechanism switched on its field, while a relay triggered the main emergency radio inside the asteroid. Presently the *Navel* switched course from the next asteroid over to Monstro.

It wasn't enough to save him—his body, anyway. But the freezebox kept what little was left alive; and when the doctor came, only the right side of a face was left to greet him in a fixed meaningless stare.

But the right lobe of Joe Winslow's brain was still alive. . . .

Benjy Tyler didn't understand about gravity.

McNulty didn't understand about Benjy not understanding.

Besides, McNulty had other things occupying his mind. The *News-Post* had a lovely story about the space jinx—he marveled at the way the jinx had killed two people almost at the same time, the other day. No, wait, they weren't killed. The docs had their brains all nice and neat in little boxes. Tinkering with 'em over at New Bellevue. Nasty stuff, doctoring. Never leave a body alone. . . .

He chuckled over his accidental witticism, then set the paper down for a moment. Time to give the dummy his mile run. Who cares about all that spacecrot anyway. Buncha people thinkin' they're better'n everybody, going off up there and leaving the real work for real people to do down here on the real world—

There was a clatter at the door and McNulty looked up, expecting to see Benjy.

A tall thin youth with blond hair caromed off the door and backpedaled into the track room.

"Bill!" McNulty said with surprise. "What's got into you?"

"What got into that Tyler bastard, you mean." Bill was highly indignant as he rubbed his arms and shoulders.

McNulty looked at him, then asked, "What did you do to him?"

"Huh?" Bill said, freshly aggrieved. "What the hell do you mean? I was only—"

"You was only deviling him, you mean," McNulty said firmly. "Now leave off him. That kid's ma is worth seven million at least, and she sure can tell when he's not been happy. And deviling him ain't making him happy."

"Aw, hell, Mac, I only tried to give him a friendly pop on the arm. He don't understand about—"

"Listen," McNulty said tiredly, "you can't jolly that kid. I tell you he don't understand *nothing*. Especially about you," he added, with what for him passed for a sneer.

He went on relentlessly. "Just for that you can run with him today. I get bored not bein' able to talk to him."

Bill shrugged. "I don't know what difference it makes, somebody runnin' with him or not."

"Listen, you achin' to be out of a job? You make plenty of money here, you can do some work for it. The kid ain't happy, nobody runnin' with him. He ain't happy, his mother knows about it. Then *she* ain't happy. She's got seven million. You run with the kid."

"Ok, ok, Mac, soothe it. But why don't we make up some exercises for him that don't wear us down so much?"

"Get going."

Bill turned to see Benjy jogging in through the door, a smile on his face, enmity forgotten, nonexistent, lost in that final trap of missing synapses.

"Run?" asked Benjy.

Bill nodded, with a sigh. "Run."

The smile became a grin. "Run!" He jogged toward the starting line of the oval track, then jogged in place waiting for Bill to join him. "Run run run run run run run run . . ." he said happily.

Bill came to the starting line and immediately Benjy began running at full speed.

"Wait a—oh, hell." Caught flat-footed, Bill was ten paces behind Benjy before he even started.

McNulty grinned broadly, then frowned, thinking it made him look like an idiot and that one idiot was enough in a day.

"Easier, he says," he muttered. "It ain't easy, thinkin' of somethin' safe enough for the poor bastard to do. Lessee . . ."

The oval track was, typically, a semi-second floor, about six meters above the first; no more than a track, six paths wide, it overhung the ground floor like a balcony, freeing extra floor area there for more equipment and room to maneuver, without having to move everything away from the track every time you wanted to have a bit of running. This pleased McNulty's orderly mind.

It also provided room for extra-level activities such as rope climbing. McNulty leaned over the track railing and grabbed a loose line, swung himself over, and handed himself down to the ground floor, dropping the last meter with a satisfying thump.

Above him came the regular pad-pad-pad of the runners, in perfect time because it distressed Benjy when the one running with him broke the tempo.

"I'd like a couple minutes inside that kid's mind to find out how it works," McNulty said aloud, knowing it made no difference if Benjy heard him.

Then he looked about him at the gym equipment he supervised. It *had* been a while since he'd given Benjy something new to do. Maybe something that didn't take so damn much supervising . . .

"Hey," came Bill's voice in a shout. "You can't do that! Mac—stop him!"

McNulty looked up.

Directly above him was the dangling rope he'd just used to climb down from the track—and Benjy was reaching out for it.

McNulty grabbed for the rope too—but Benjy had it now, and was putting his weight on it.

"If I pull on it now, it might pull him over, make him fall," Mac said to himself, and his chest gave him several sharp pangs. "Where's that bastard Bill gotten to?"

He looked around and saw Bill running toward Benjy, who had apparently outdistanced him half the length of the track.

In clumsy imitation of the man he'd watched play the new game, Benjy held onto the rope with his hands and let the rope and his torso swing out over the six-meter drop—while his feet were still entangled in the railing bars.

"Bill, you damn fool, grab his legs," Mac shouted, feeling his back sweating and his mind already numbed, unable to think of anything at all to do, and scared—so scared.

Benjy began to let his hands slide down the rope,

not understanding what was happening, and the burning sensation made him relax his hands.

Like a pendulum his body, headfirst, began swinging down under the floor of the track. The constriction on his legs now hurt even more than his hands had, and his legs began thrashing wildly to free themselves.

Just as Bill reached the kicking legs, they untangled themselves from the bars and disappeared from his sight.

"Wheeeeeeeeee!" Benjy said, and then his body hit the oak floor of the gymnasium, forehead first, completing the wreckage nature had endowed him with.

CHAPTER THREE

PARKER RAISED his hand. "Just a moment, Dr Brian. I want you to know that I understand the difficulty of your position—just as much as I understand the difficulty of the position of those poor bastards you're going to operate on."

Dr John Brian, Chief of First and Second Divisions, Microsurgery, New Bellevue, sat back in his chair. "It is a fantastic opportunity to learn, sir; I want you to understand that, and understand it clearly. I'm prepared to be reasonably cooperative with you, as long as you understand the nature of my commitment in this matter."

Parker smiled oddly, and knew that Jailyn Rost would have instantly been put on her guard by it. The thought was a pang that went through him, then stayed on and continued as a painful background sensation.

"I want a story, Dr Brian. It's the old 'only my job' routine, I suppose, or sounds that way to you. But I have a personal commitment in this matter too, as you phrase it, and it's not entirely because I was with her just before it . . . happened."

Once more Leslie Parker tasted for a brief poignant moment the memory of the beauty of Jailyn Rost, and once more superimposed immediately on that memory came the thought of what was left of her being immured in the husk of a nineteen-year-old idiot—and with some damn fool of a careless multiwave technician, at that, to share the body with.

His face must have shown more than he had intended, for Dr Brian smiled thinly. "Mr Parker, it is clear that you accept the logical necessity of what I am going to do—and that you do *not* accept it, emotionally. I will not speculate on any emotional ties that might exist between you and Miss Rost, but it is obvious that your concern runs deeper than I, as a medical researcher and practitioner, dare to take cognizance of."

Parker frowned and shook his head. "I read all the releases, doctor. Immune-reaction tests, compatibility factors, stable and similar genetic dispositions, and a great deal of other matters that I am going to have to take up the study of before I grasp their significance. These three people are similar enough to accept each other's proteins, with proper suppressants of course. The chance that another body will be available that either Miss Rost or this Winslow fellow could utilize for transplant is—"

"Is possible, Mr Parker, but not in any sense likely. I cannot maintain either of them alive outside a body for more than another week at the utmost, before irreversible basic damage sets in."

Parker waved his hand. "I know that. What concerns me is the uncertainty of the whole affair. I am a professional in my own field, as you are in yours, doctor; and in my case it means I know how to research those necessary background facts that make conversations such as this more meaningful than the customary exchange of platitudinous awarenesses of each other's position. For instance, most people think of brain transplants—insofar as they think of them at all—as routine, even though it's been only eleven years since the first one. There have been hundreds since then, running the gamut from moderate success to rather revolting failure.

I know a little about the Boardman experiments, also, and—"

Dr Brian's face stiffened; harsh vertical lines appeared, and for the first time he looked his fifty years. "No reputable medical man will discuss the Boardman matter—none that I know of, at any rate."

Parker's smile was not a smile any longer, though his lips were curved as though nothing had changed. "You needn't say anything, doctor—just be aware that I know more of the story than, it seems, makes you happy."

Dr Brian took a deep breath. "Boardman was a sensationalist; his experiments do not deserve serious attention. Since you seem to feel the possibility of an affinity between his attitudes and mine, I will point out that my primary concern is that my patients come through this ordeal safely. The knowledge is secondary. If we can start with this as a point of common understanding between us . . . ?"

"I concede that we have been sparring, doctor, and that you have much better things to do than bandy words with—"

"Not at all. You knew Miss Rost and you deal in explaining intricate matters to the public, for a living. I would rather deal with you than a horde of arrogant ignoramuses. But, sir, I will not be badgered."

Now Parker sat back. It was with some surprise that he discovered he had been sitting tensely rigid, as if the archaic Saarinen chair were wired for high voltage and the doctor was toying with its switch. "Very well, then. I would like to follow you along as closely as you will allow—as closely as the medical requirements of the situation will allow—and I will refrain from arguing with you when you judge I would be a dangerous hindrance. By the same token, however, if intern privileges—"

"You will have modified intern privileges, Mr Parker. I am aware that you are a responsible man and that you understand what such privileges entail on your part."

"Modified?"

Dr Brian had a thin smile too. "Modified, Mr Parker. I will permit no one except staff to be involved in any direct contact with the subjects under any circumstances whatsoever at any time until such time as I in my personal judgment consider such contact harmless."

Parker stood up. "In other words, you deny me most of my story. But," he went on before Dr Brian's smile widened, "I will accept your terms anyway."

Parker considered it to his credit that Dr Brian's broadening smile did not narrow back down at the acceptance.

"Then that's settled; excellent." Hands reached out, shook perfunctorily. "If you will forgive me, I must prepare for the first open demonstration. You can process through and be at the central operating room in less than an hour, I believe."

Parker shrugged. "I presume so."

"Then I shall see you there. In the meantime, I have much to do. . . ."

"—and then there was the new problem presented in this particular case, of course." Dr Brian had been addressing assembled interns seated in the rotunda surrounding the central operating area. Parker sat among the interns, wearing a shapeless garment three sizes too big for him that hindered his note-taking.

"I have already detailed my reasoning behind implanting both of the single surviving lobes simultaneously, without making the interconnections between them until now. Well, not simultaneous implantation; the Winslow lobe, being male, was appropriately implanted first, observed *in situ* for unforeseen reactions, and then we proceeded with the female lobe. Utilizing heavier suppressant levels than usual, we avoided any conflict that might stem from this, hm, unusual situation, and no untoward problems have as yet occurred.

"This being the case, we are now to proceed with connecting the two lobes with each other. Following this will come many months of painstaking work with scanning monitors and suppressant balances, as we allow the two personalities slowly to become aware of their new situation, of their new body, of each other, and so forth."

Dr Brian attempted a comradely chuckle that became a lonely echo in the upper reaches of the chamber; the interns were too intent on following the preliminary work Dr Brian's assistants were already engaged in while the chief microsurgeon lectured.

"Hm, well. You will have observed on your screens that we are going to go at this problem in basically the same fashion as any routine trunk connections. I think it's time to bring the hand camera, nurse—over here, so the microdetail work can be followed . . . right."

Dr Brian inserted his hands into the microsurgical gloves and flexed his fingers a few times.

On a hundred personal threedee screens the interns watched the microfingers flex with Dr Brian's movements. Nurses then arrayed microtools within range, and Dr Brian cleared his throat. "Now," he said, knowing his words were quite unnecessary, "we can proceed with the first phase of this part of the operation. . . ."

Jailyn in darkness and silence, tumbleweed thoughts bouncing occasionally above suppressants into flavors and fragments of dreams . . .

Sleep . . .

Dreamt of a velvet dress, my dear, so sweet . . .

Arms, legs, body so heavy . . .

Danced with the boys till night met the morning and sipped champagne till I slept at noon . . .

"It's too quiet."

But no sound, and the thick feel of tongue slack in

a dry mouth, awake, dreaming of being awake, awake
and dreaming of being awake and dreaming . . .

"Where am I?" Tongue rasping on teeth. No
sound?

Stars danced in the spangled bright sky and danced
and danced and I'd giggle again as I did when first
the brilliant bubbles tickled my throat and the boys
flashed warm inebriated smiles and the sachet between
my breasts with spicy clove hints of

"My teeth are wrong."

That's silly. And why can't I hear myself talk?

Am I talking?

Am I dreaming?

I'm in no night no day nothing but the knowledge
of nothing (sensory sensory sensory deprivation deprivation remember it's only a) and the sound of my
unvoiced words echoing in the back of . . . what?

"Where am I?"

Wha—can't move! feel? anything?

Ha, taste of something: fear. Begin there?

Logicalsensorydeprivation concept, hold that/there
is nothing to fear/o

         h! I can't feel anything, I can't do
anything, I can't even worry about it, am I, except
my tongue or yes I feel my tongue, and

                            dreams of
strange teeth? Strange teeth. That's ridiculous; a
strange thought to lie between a woman's teeth,
ridiculous; my lady, you are not well, and what is
more, you are not well, and what is more—

If the mind is well, remember: the body can be
healed, oh, they tell us, oh, my lady . . .

Splitting asunder . . .

Like an ear? No, cold memories of warmly lost
virginity—but wasn't there . . .

The central imploder; there was an adjustment to
make; another concept, hold that. Imploder. Adjustment.

But there'd been something wrong—wasn't there? Head so heavy, cannot think.

Postoperative shock.

Grin with relief and closed eyes still, grin—with lips strangely tight and . . . was I hurt? Hurt? Hurt? Of course, or I'd understand . . .

Understand how I could be still dreaming waking tasting strange teeth with odd tight lips, imploder blast hurting—

Hurt? By an imploder? Hurt? Be atoms ashes dissolution of all flesh utterly with my memories orbiting Mars; oh, if something should go wrong and an imploder blew—an implo—

Ah, dear God! A transplant!

Tongue stirred again.

Not my mouth.

My body never so heavy, never so—

Breath swept finally up over untrained vocal cords in a harsh heavy scream as Jailyn Rost allowed herself at last for one brief mental glimpse to sense the sturdy masculinity of her body, hair, muscles, somberer hormones, legs, nightmare at the phallus impossibly just there . . .

And soft half-dreamless sleep drifted up over her like a veil of snow over a harsh wasteland. . . .

For Joe Winslow the transition was sudden, more controlled, clear; hormonal balances stirred no deep contradictions.

Sleep one moment, and awareness of darkness, silence, and heavy body the next.

He shuddered momentarily at some nameless memory of a hideous dream about an ear, an ear that split and poured out horrors inexplicably sexual; then he had control of himself, remembering there had been an accident.

Therefore he was in a hospital; that was clear to him.

There! That was easy, he told himself.

Now, why can't I see and hear?

Well, what kind of an accident?

Funny dream that was, about drinking champagne in the morning. Can't make any sense out of that at all. . . .

Maybe the accident did something to my body they haven't been able to fix yet. Reinjured my spine, something like that—but they had my eyes open and I was talking within twenty-four hours after that one.

Mouth tastes funny.

Feels funny. Whoops, don't get carried away! Why can't I move my arm?

There.

Twitched my hand, anyway.

Make a fist.

Ok.

Make a fist with the other hand.

Ok.

Clasp hands.

Ok.

Those aren't my hands!

He held his breath a moment, then exhaled slowly, noticing as he did that his rather narrow nose now seemed much broader; it was easier to breathe. . . .

Transplant?

The only answer; well . . .

A wave of shock hit him; his mind writhed seething with oceanic fears for a cosmic instant

                                      —then dropped

back sharply.

He recognized suppressant effects; *so.* He was being monitored; *so.* He was being looked after; *so* what did he have to worry about . . . ?

Put my brain into another man's body, will they? Anger—illogical. Can't get angry anyway; they'll swamp me with neuroquench.

The multiwave blast—it must have burned away so much of . . . of me there wasn't enough left to try to save. Except my life, except my life, except—

Lucky me; my suit froze me up in time, saved the old skull. Be a bit harder getting used to than a broken back, eh? Old brain, favorite brain, companion of my youth . . . now and in the hour of the death of the rest of me . . .

His mind drifted away from contemplating the alien body he was now a part of.

Like death, now—transplanted heads . . .

No man thinks it's going to happen to him; he recognized he was musing bemusedly now, drowsy, feeling sleepy now; *we got problems, Joe, baby; they may not call you Mr Winslow any more, when you come out of this one. . . .*

He tried to make his voice work; only a croak emerged.

Then blankness wiped over his mind, a film dissolve into peaceful oblivion, almost dreamless. . . .

"It was hardly necessary to make the effort of predicting which one would find such a new situation the least difficult to adjust to. Winslow's got a lot of natural stability, and he knows the microsurgical routine—it was a second cousin of mine who put his spine back together again, oh, hardly more than six months ago. He isn't finding it difficult to trust his safety in the new situation. Miss Rost, now, is having her problems."

Parker could not stand the seductive curves of the old Saarinen any longer. He jumped to his feet, alarmed as he did so at the unsuspectedly high tension he had developed in the last . . . how long had it been?

"Dr Brian, I am not certain that you have been entirely frank with me," he said on impulse. "I for one cannot see why they should have spent such a long time now, almost entirely in deep suppressant-induced sleep. Months, it's been. I've watched your computer readouts, learned to translate some of the implications of all those jagged lines, seen threedees of them during those brief moments you've allowed one of them to come awake. Just what do you think you're accomplishing? Surely the microhealing process does not require all this?"

"I thought I had explained near the beginning of the first lecture," Dr Brian said testily. "Why, we don't know, but the new brain in the old body seems to make most of its adjustments well below conscious levels—*well* below. Were our subjects conscious for any significant level of time, it could only interfere with the natural process in which the two previously alien lifeforms, as it were, learn to live together in what should be a reasonably perfect symbiosis. Breathing, for instance. Whichever we have awake, the breathing is handled with no difficulty—now. I'll admit much of that is handled by what's left of Benjy's midbrain and cerebellum, but—"

"My good doctor," Parker said, not bothering to hide his sarcasm. "I am not entirely lacking in knowledge of the wisdom of modern science. It has limped back and ahead of itself in many wonderful ways since the setbacks of the plaguewars, not to mention the Changes. I cannot see that, for instance, permitting me a few minutes' conversation with . . . with Miss Rost would seriously upset her ability to breathe, doctor."

"Indeed." Dr Brian stood. "The judgmental prerogatives in this matter happen to be entirely in my hands. *Entirely.* And I do not wish to introduce any additional outside stresses until we have learned all we can about the situation while the situation remains substantially untouched by nonclinical stimuli. Pardon my stilted diction; I am attempting to convey a difficult concept and at the same time I am attempting to keep from losing my temper."

There was a light triple tap on the door, and after a moment it opened. Chief Nurse Kim entered, crossed to Dr Brian's desk, and laid a folder on it, all without a word.

Parker added it up, and spoke. "Now that you're beginning to lift the suppressants on interactions between the two brains, I shall start coming round again every day. You are being quite cooperative, doctor, for which I and my employers thank you. You must forgive my impatience when in the natural arrogance of the professional newsgatherer I try for more than is good—good for me, or good for you, I will not judge. At any rate, I shall see you tomorrow."

Dr Brian picked up the folder and muttered an acknowledgment as Parker left.

"I'm . . . scared, doctor," Chief Nurse Alicia Kim said. "About the girl, about . . . Jailyn. She's obviously building a minor psychosis about the male body—she's panicked every time we've let her up far enough for her to fully realize she's now in a man's—"

Dr Brian sat back, folder in hand, and smiled up. "Alicia," he said, his voice calm and gentle, "we have all the time in the world. Every case we've handled so far has made it through eventually, using precisely the techniques we're using now—allowing for the extra problem in this case."

"Extra problem!" The nurse dropped into the Saarinen antique, and sighed. "In one strange man's body and next-door neighbor to another man!"

She unconsciously smoothed the bodice of her spotless white uniform in a gesture Dr Brian was well familiar with; once more he contentedly realized she was a fine figure of a woman, and only in her thirties.

"I mean," she went on, "I don't think I realized till now just what that would mean. I'm a woman too," she went on after only a slight pause, and Dr Brian amusedly noticed her blushing slightly, "and . . . and I don't know whether *I* could remain . . . sane, if they—if *you*, Dr Brian—did that to me.

"I mean, well, why couldn't you have given her a female body and him the Tyler body?"

"You know as well as I do," Brian said, glowering unaccustomedly at his nurse. "We can't keep minds sane when the brain is just floating about in nutrient solution. And we need subjects with a reasonably good matchup of macromolecular types." He shrugged, genuinely unconcerned. "We had no choice—and the learning opportunities are providing us with a great deal of valuable new—"

"I hadn't thought about . . . about being a . . . a girl in . . . in a boy's . . . body . . ."

His nurse had not precisely broken down into hysterical tears, but she was under strain, that was clear; she shook silently, and tears were now leaking down her face. Mental regression too, he noted, using terms like "girl" and "boy" for full-grown adults.

"I don't quite understand," he said, a bit stiffly through the astonishment he felt at the woman's reaction. "I'm sure it wouldn't bother me, were my brain to be placed in a woman's body—an attractive woman's body, at least!" He tried a chuckle.

Alicia looked up and stared at him, quite forgetting her tears.

He was astonished to realize he was blushing; and he found himself coughing in a futile attempt to cover up. "Perhaps we'd better get back to the scan integrations." He looked down at the folder in his hand, aware of purse scrabbling across the desk from him; there was a pause, then a characteristic "sniff," and he looked up. The stimutranq worked fast, and Alicia had already dried her incredible tears. He grunted with satisfaction.

She became efficiency in white. "The scanner indicates that the crossover flashes are so far accepted by Winslow without question, if with momentary puzzlement. Doctor, this strikes me as crucial—how are you

going to tell them that there's *two* of them in that
skull?"

"I think," said Dr Brian with obvious reluctance,
"that is a problem they're going to have to find the
answer to, long before we dare to bring them up
long enough to speak to them."

Blackness lifted; how many times before?

Jailyn Rost tried to blink and could not move.

*Dreaming again? What is this kind of endless black
reality where I see nothing, know nothing, can learn
nothing . . . I must be dreaming, but so long, so
long?*

*Her mind wandered, searching fruitlessly for ob-
jective reality.*

Why?

*Why am I searching? Why haven't they brought
me up and told me?*

Is it worse than I surmise?

*No, can't be; that's out. The body must be
healthy or they wouldn't have transplanted me into
it; they don't transplant into dying bodies. The body
—no, he—is healthy.*

*This thought, revising from neuter to male came
immediately, and immediately her mind sheered
away again.*

*So the body must be all right. All right. No worry
there. No problem. So . . .*

*So why am I still adrift in limbo? Why can't I
open my eyes, move my legs, clench my—*

*The right hand moved, I felt it move! But . . .
did I move it?*

*Then the left hand moved, clenched, and in a
moment both hands moved toward each other, and
clasped . . .*

*Moments later they relaxed and fell back at rest
position.*

That has happened before, she thought; but the

thought was blanketed by another: How did I do that!

For a moment all thought was drowned in animal panic; then her intellect asserted itself.

Automatic; it must have been some automatic reflex of this body, she thought. Either they haven't hooked me up completely yet, or they're using suppressants on me so strongly *I can't tie into the hookups.*

She felt an urge to smile then, and a sort of weight lifted from her.

Sort of a signal? she thought. Perhaps! Maybe they were trying to tell me about the suppressants. There's . . . something . . . something I've got to do, on my own, in here, with no way to communicate.

I wonder what?

And how can I do it?

Joe Winslow woke and pondering the interesting fact that he had once more dreamed he was a woman.

No . . . not quite that . . .

It was hard to put a name to it. There had been strangeness in the woman dream . . . that was it! Not that he was dreaming he was a woman—he had *heard a woman's dream!*

Odd by-product of a transplant. Could understand it if they'd put me in a woman's body. Boy! Wouldn't that have been something!

He felt an urge to grin. Women are fun, he thought. It's fun to watch them, fun to communicate with them, fun to make love with them.

Q.E.D. It would be fun to be a woman!

No, correction; it would be fun to have a man's mind in a woman's body.

Like lesbians, he thought; men are fascinated by lesbians, still repelled by male homosexuals . . . why?

Because lesbians are attracted sexually to women, so that their sexual activities are inherently interesting to males. While if one is not sexually interested in males, their sexual activities are not interesting . . .

Wheee, deep thoughts tonight! Or is it day? God, it's quiet in here!

That dream . . . a woman. Oh, to be a woman now that spring is here!

Oh, shut up. Talk sense. Here you are trapped in someone else's skull while they're off . . .

Which brings up the interesting question of who I am these days. . . .

I wish I could scratch my head . . . it always used to help me think. Dammit, doctor, let me scratch my head so I can think! I know you're out there with your scanners and your theories! Why are you giving me such a hard time?

Now, then, there's a good question.

Maybe the doc has to give me a hard time.

Why?

But—it's just a simple transplant. I know about them, there's been hundreds . . .

Unless . . .

Maybe part of my brain was damaged, too?

So they can't hook me up to everything?

That, I'll have to think about.

Later. Sleep now.

Sleep now.

Sle

The Miles High blasted down through the midnight sky.

"Jimmy, why are we landing on Mount Everest?"

Jailyn was giddy, giddy with the weight and weightlessness that always alternated through Jimmy's landing patterns. Jimmy knew she always got a kick, did it on purpose, fire him some day, fire . . .

"It's the Skycycle Gang, Missy Rost," came Jimmy's voice, Oxford accent accentuated by the intercom.

"The what?"

"The Skycycle Gang. They're after us. Or we're after them; hard to say, Missy Rost."

Jailyn furrowed her brow and leaned against a bulkhead.

It gave way beneath the pressure of her body and she and it toppled slowly to the floor.

Dreamily she bounded to her feet and started wafting her way through the winding long dark narrow open-mesh tunnel to the heart of the multiHigh's cabin—

Dreamily she wondered where the tunnel came from, no winding tunnels in the Miles High, like an access route to a multiwave tuner core . . .

I don't understand this dream at all, she thought, as weightless she drifted around through the meaningless winding tunnel.

"Why is the Skycycle Gang after us?"

"Missy Rost, we're being followed," came Jimmy Tungo's voice; and she blinked, finding herself in the control cabin of her ship.

"What is it, Jimmy?" She was looking out on the night sky beyond the ship, which had paused, hovering impossibly above the eternal plume bannering proudly off the top of Everest.

Above them, clearly visible on the upper screens, a large object was hurtling down at them.

"What is it?" she gasped.

"Planetoid. Meteor. Asteroid. Whale. I don't know," said Jimmy, his voice calm. "The artwork makes it look a little like a Disney—classic inking. Almost Krigstein. You know."

She nodded.

I do? she thought incuriously. Lordy, what a strange comic strip this is! I wish I could tell my kitten about this . . . remember, you are only a dream.

What?

A pun, and a bad one . . . but I never make bad puns. . . .

"We're trapped, Missy Rost! Trapped! Between the Skycycle Gang and the mountain and the whale, the asteroid, the . . ."

Mount Everest ripped apart with a thundering roar.

Blackness poured out in a never-ending stream and Jailyn Rost lost consciousness. . . .

"Lot of work ahead," said Dr John Brian. "A *lot* of work. . . ."

CHAPTER FOUR

"I am Jailyn Rost."

The voice was husky, soft—and sounded infinitely lost.

Eight hours had gone by since the beginning of the first experiment in lifting the suppressants, and Dr Brian had spent the time making a difficult decision.

And now the body of Benjy Tyler lay in a bed-hospital blinking up at Dr Brian and whispering, over and over, "I am Jailyn Rost. *I am Jailyn Rost!*"

"Yes," said Dr Brian finally. "You don't really need to doubt that."

"I am Jailyn Rost!"

But this time the voice spoke even lower.

"You are Jailyn Rost," said Dr. Brian, "and you are already aware that you have been in an accident that a few years ago would have done you in completely."

Rather astonishingly, the Tyler head nodded slightly.

Dr Brian essayed a grin. "You'd be, hm, looking around for a body to reincarnate into—you might say we've spared you the trouble, done it for you, complete with your old memories."

"Thanks," said the whisper, and Dr Brian could not detect either gratitude or irony in it. "How many transplants have you done before that involved sex switch?"

Dr Brian studied sensor readouts, gleaning little from

them while testing for the last time the web of evasive words he'd preconstructed for this scene.

"There have only been a dozen brain transplants in the last two years," he said. "They don't happen very often, for a variety of reasons. Even with the freeze-box, brain cells deteriorate rapidly enough so that, unless a suitable donor body is available within less than two weeks, no operation is possible. Furthermore, you must understand that most countries have imposed stringent restrictions on any transplants; they do not permit major organ transplants without a set of familial releases that . . . well, I'm sure you understand. It seems many people think it inhuman to, er, strive officiously to keep alive, or however the line goes. And how do *you* feel about it, by the way?"

His manner was intended to give the impression he had just thought of the question; but in fact he was almost certain the answer would not be negative, long before he decided to ask it. The mind was remarkably sensitive to some of the energizing drugs routinely used in transplants—drugs he himself often thought dangerously close to mind-warping drugs that sent a certain percentage of the population each year out into the country to rot, or whatever they did out there. At any rate, Jailyn Rost had enough in her system, or rather in the Tylerbody system, to keep her away from any protracted thoughts of suicide.

"I am alive, and I am Jailyn Rost," came the whisper; then at last a defiant note came through. "And for now, at least, that's good enough for me! But you did not answer my question."

He smiled reassuringly down at . . . her, and in the same moment blinked with the realization that he had actually thought of this strapping young male body as "her." There was a lot to think about in this, he realized; but this was not the time for it.

"Jailyn," he said, noticing with gratification the clear indications of muscular relaxation as "she" absorbed the casually conversational validation of her identity, "if you think I am being evasive, I can tell you that all this information is thoroughly and completely a matter of record, except for the records destroyed down in Capetown. As for the remaining records, so far all but two transplants were same-sex, and the two exceptions were male brains into female bodies.

"True, one of these latter died shortly thereafter—from other and irrelevant causes, I assure you, not correlated with the transplant itself but with the original accident that had made the transplant necessary in the first place.

"The other male brain turned out to be quite pleased with his new body—he was, however, an unsuspected pathological homosexual, heavily imprinted. So I must confess that I cannot offer you any deep conclusions from past experiences. However, I assure you we had no alternative in your case but to take the one body we had available."

Dr Brian cleared his throat; then found himself in a coughing spasm before he could go on. "I do not hide this fact from you, you see. You are, hm, unique, or this case is."

There was a long low sigh from the Tylerbody, and "she" closed "her" eyes. "Then that might explain those strange, strange dreams . . ."

"Do they bother you?" asked Dr Brian, assuming a momentarily strict doctor-patient manner and ostentatiously frowning at his lightpen, poised over his portable readout plate.

"Why, yes . . . but not unbearably, I suppose. It hadn't occurred to me that a transplant might involve the possibility of memories left over from the previous . . ."

Dr Brian was certain she had been about to say "body" but could not bring herself to say it.

If so, that was good to know, too; she was a little more squeamish than he had expected—and thus his judgment not to let her realize directly the dual nature of the transplant, just yet, seemed confirmed as sound.

He made a tiny adjustment on the bed-hospital monitor that was part of the readout plate, carefully, so that she could not see him. It was better not to pursue this line of argument too much farther, so he released a small quantity of soporific into her bloodstream via the remote.

Presently the Tylereyes opened again, heavy-lidded this time.

"I feel tired, doctor; perhaps we can resume this conversation at a later time . . . I have much to learn, but I'll have to . . . take it . . . easy. . . ."

Tylereyes closed.

Dr Brian made some additional adjustments in the suppressant balances, then rubbed his hands over his face in exhaustion.

Nurse Kim stepped forward. "*You* need rest, doctor," she said briskly. "Come away, now."

"I'll bring her up more and more often," he said absently, "and leave her there for longer and longer times. Must start training the motor-nerve controls for heavier activities—and then there's Winslow. Can't keep him asleep and dreaming *too* long, but if he doesn't dream neither of them will learn . . ."

"Come *away*, doctor," Nurse Kim said again, touching his arm, then grasping it with feminine firmness to prove her seriousness.

"Hm, yes," he said, turning to her with an abstracted look in his eyes. "Dreams . . ."

Dreams.

Jailyn did not get upset when her next dream was obviously a male one, partly because that part of her mind she was not consciously aware of was getting used to its situation, and partly because that part of her conscious mind that was somewhat aware of her dreams was getting used to *its* situation. An additional calming factor was Nurse Kim's recalibration of suppressant patterns, keying in more sharply at sexual anxieties when they were detected above a certain level.

She knew it wasn't *her* dream, practically from the start, this time. There had been others she couldn't bear to remember . . . or had they been no worse than this? In the sleep-drugged state, half-aware she was dreaming another's dreams, she observed the succession of events with a detachment which, under ordinary circumstances, fully awake, would have greatly alarmed her.

"All right, I'll take you and you and you," she found herself saying.

She was not disquieted to find the male she seemed to be, here in this caliph's palace, was older than the body she thought she'd glimpsed in her previous dreams. Asleep, it only seemed curious that these things should be, curious only that she should be dreaming a man's strange dream and know she was dreaming.

She saw the dancing girls, in a line before the man she was; and found she was lying on a couch of tasteless red plush, fully clothed in some nondescript technician's uniform.

But the room . . . silk hangings everywhere, and ivory fretwork, an Arabian palace filled with a faint sound of cymbals and lutes and with strange perfumes. "Odd," she thought, noticing the scent, "odors, in a dream?"

The dancing girls moved together toward the couch, bodies seductively swaying . . . drawing her eyes irresistibly to them despite her puzzled interest in the gaudy surroundings. She wanted to frown in concentration; but the man in coveralls she was dreaming simply laughed.

"First, dancing and singing," he/she said, cheerfully, "and later maybe we'll all mess around a bit!"

Damn powerful memories lurking around in this husk of a body, Jailyn thought dreamily, and her puzzlement increased. *Even a little sense of humor left over for me, not that I need it—or maybe I do!*

Immediately the girls were naked now, clicking their fingers and dancing round the floor, feet and hands and arms intricately interweaving, breasts swaying, nipples on some already aroused.

Jailyn tried to look away again, but against her will her eyes caressed the delightful forms enthusiastically—and her body was reacting.

Panic hit her then; her new and never-forgotten manhood stiffened, responding, the male body was naked now, and reaching out for the nearest girl, slender and young and smiling—panic, and the dream winked out and she dropped into unknowingness. . . .

"Now this one is a *real* dream," Joe Winslow was thinking to himself as the girls swirled about the room. "I didn't get 'em like this, grubbing around on that damned asteroid."

His eyes caressed the delightful forms enthusiastically, his body reacting automatically. Finding himself suddenly naked, he thought *What the hell,* and started up to reach out for the nearest girl, slender and young and smiling—

—when he was suddenly hit with a totally unexpected surge of utter revulsion, followed almost immediately by a sense of *shifting* that deeply disquieted him in its strangeness, a feeling of somehow dropping away into nothingness . . . he looked puzzledly at the dancing girls as they began fading away.

He blinked and was awake, lying in a bed-hospital, with an attractive nurse on the far side of the room absorbed in studying the readout panel of a large computer monitor console.

"You can't fool me," he said aloud, surprising himself as much as the nurse, who suppressed a little shriek of alarm and turned to him as if touched by a lash, an oddly guilty look on her face.

"You've got me plugged into this bed-hospital," he went on, the "what the hell" feeling still strong from the dream, "and you're obviously working me over. Why?"

He found his mouth was dry, and found unfamiliar salivary glands unwilling to work at the half-conscious touch of old commands. He sighed and wondered if they'd ever work for him properly, or if he'd just have to get used to a dry mouth for the rest of his life.

"You're not supposed to be awake," said the nurse, accusingly, hospital habit taking over. "I'd better put you back to sleep before the doctor—"

"Why don't you just call the doctor in here, now that I'm awake?" The saliva still wouldn't come; his new mouth tasted like desert-grown cotton. Anger began to build up from mere resentments.

"Yes," he went on, "call the doctor. I find my mind here is crammed full of all sorts of, oh, fascinating questions about my new job here; and whatever is up, it's got a lot to do with my strange, strange dreams."

Nurse Kim hesitated only briefly, knowing how hard it had been to get Dr Brian away and to sleep. Then she reached for the control that would add suppressants into the Winslow lobe's blood supply and put it into deeper sleep.

"Hold on there," Joe said, alarmed. "Now, I feel great. Let me look around a minute, will ya? Back from the dead, and all? What's your hurry? I want to . . ."

"Zonk thee," Nurse Kim said, after Joe went back under, cheerfully mixing her archaicisms. She'd goofed there—first overreacting to the Winslow dream's sexual content and what it seemed to be doing to Jailyn Rost.

But then in adding suppressants to the Rost lobe and in attempting to balance that with wakeners for Winslow, she'd overdone the wakeners.

She sighed; Dr. Brian wouldn't like that. He's wanted

Jailyn to get in as much conscious time with the Tylerbody as possible, before bringing Winslow up.

She was tired, that was it. And she'd put in as much
time as the doctor, after all. She sighed again, making
her decision, and began flicking controls on the console
to standby deepsleep.

The breathing from the bed-hospital regularized,
deepened; the readout plate indicated only subconscious integrating activity, hardly more intense than
average, considering the jolt of sexual awarenesses that
had just upset things.

"No more dreams for you tonight," she said, as she
stood up.

But Chief Nurse Kim was wrong.

During tedious later experiments, it was found that
the two lobes had a natural tendency to continue each
other in a low-level dream state. Each lobe, functioning with its own normal electrochemical activity, had
a slight but detectable electromagnetic field.

And since, inside what was left of Benjy Tyler's skull,
there were halves of two brains each with its own field,
even when asleep they impinged on each other. . . .

. . . greyness . . . awareness . . . floating . . . drifting
. . . sleeping . . . drifting . . . drifting . . . bump—

bump? whazzat?

*archetypical shapes like ancestors two four eight six-
teen thirtytwo sixtyfour onehundredtwentyeight two-
hun-*

bump? whazzat? ancestors? hullo ancestors what's
up?

*dunno, dunno, no, no, not me, they are the ances-
tors, over there, dim gray shapes in the mists, only two
of them or are there three all told*

then that's ok

RELAXED CONTENTMENT BENJY NOT ALONE NO MORE
NOT ALONE NO MORE NO MORE

what!

I had a Greatuncle Benjamin once, but

no I didn't

yes I did

no

I must be dreaming to myself. See here, Benjamin Winslow his name was, remember? He gave me a jockstrap for Christmas once when I was seven, made my folks mad but he just laughed. Sure, old Uncle Ben, never forget old Uncle Ben, and you know, I never did find out if the old guy was queer, or just had a weird sense of humor . . .

lordy how I do run on, no Winslows in the family, who's Benjy?

I dunno, who's Benjy? Uncle Ben never was called Benjy. Good question. Benjy?

PEACEJOY BENJY HAPPY SLEEPY NOT ALONE GOT FRIENDS NOW TO THINKANDDO CONTENTMENTJOYPEACE-HAPPY.

Whew! Those aren't words, but they aren't Uncle Ben, either. Ol' body, I guess; not friend of my youth but . . . I ain't got no body . . . but I *do.*

Tension apprehension and dissension as the book says, I never had an Uncle Ben. If I wasn't a big girl now, I'd say I want my mommy . . .

Who's a big girl now?

You gotta rub it in? I'm just happy Benjy is happy—whoever Benjy is.

BENJY ME, UHHHH . . .

BENJY US.

You got a point there, friend, or my name ain't Joe Winslow!

Jailyn Rost.

Joe Winslow.

Pleased to meet you. I have this feeling that about now I should be screaming.

Me too. What are you doing in here, rooting about in my dreams and whatnot?

I don't know, but I'm beginning to think that hos-

pitals and their damned conscious dreaming was the most dangerous thing developed in the first half of the twenty-first century, I'll tell you that.

Heh. You? Who are you?

's impolite to ask one to have more tea when there isn't any, y'know. . . .

Alice? Thought the name was Jailyn?

You're literary, anyway, so I know you're just a figment of my dream. Presently I shall snap my dreamlike fingers and you will go away and . . .

Not on your sweet ass do I go away!

Oh!

I mean, this is my bunk and you . . . well, *sorry* spare my blushes. Forgot there was a lady present, and—

BENJY SAY *don't fight*

```
  h              h
   u              u
    h              h
     h              h
```

Whew!

Ugh!

I dunno what's going on, but I don't want any more of *that*.

Ok, we won't fight.

Ok, truce.

Who are you?

Who are *you*?

I don't like this dream anymore.

Lady, I'm not so sure it's a dream. . . .

. . . what? hey, there, manthoughts, you, Benjy, thinking at me, who are you? how can you think without a brain?

BENJY DUNNO. BRAIN? THINK? BENJY HERE. BENJY HAPPY. BENJY LISTEN. BENJY LIKE TO LISTEN.

Now, then, lady, observe: there wasn't a single coherent thought there; it was just shadow concepts, translated into words by my forebrain——or yours, if you exist. Got it? Damn clever, these mad scientists. . . .

I am going to stop talking to myself, now.

AWWWW

Lady——

I don't like being addressed as "lady" by myself, even if I am one. Was one. Am one. Damn!

There's a trick to it, you know, conscious dreaming. Not everybody knows it, or of it, not even doctors. Why, back when I was to college with a country-people type, he was telling me all about it; it must have stuck even though I didn't pay that much attention——

What country people told me what? Whew, I've got to stop imagining these things, or they'll never let me——

BENJY SLEEP NOW

Hey, what's——I want to find out what's——

Yeah, don't do that, whatever you're——there's too——

BENJY SLEEP NOW

CHAPTER FIVE

"Now THEN, Miss Kim, didn't you set the console for deepsleep programing before you left last night?"

Dr Brian stood by the window pouring in artificial sunlight—the Tylerbody room being on the tenth underground level—glancing through the computer's summary of the night's activity.

"Why, yes, doctor; see, the settings are right there on deepsleep. Surely the readout confirms—what's the matter?"

"Well, look here—obvious indications of a good deal of activity, not long after you left. And from all *three* of them, which is . . ." Dr Brian's voice trailed off, as abstractedly he looked once more at the readout.

"All *three* of them?" Miss Kim, still upset at possible criticism of her carelessness with the sexual dreaming, had not immediately grasped Dr Brians' words.

"Oh, yes, it's quite clear. The Benjymind was probably not contributing much on a very high level, but it was much more active last night than I've ever seen it previously. Well, now, I wonder whether they've already figured out . . . hm. Bring up Miss Rost, if you will, please, Alicia. I think I'll do a little verbal probing. Then, if she's adjusted to the transplant situation as well as she seems to, this might be the time that the rest of the information won't hit her too hard. . . ."

Miss Kim frowned slightly. "Do you really think it's wise this early, so far ahead of schedule?"

Dr Brian grinned unexpectedly. "She doesn't seem to have been quite as upset by the sex-switch aspect of it as you were, eh?"

She flushed prettily and turned away to the control panel. He *had* noticed the earlier . . . misjudgment.

"Bringing up Miss Rost," she said in a professional manner; then, "Yes, you're probably right, there, doctor. I'm sorry about—"

"Huh. Never mind sorry, it doesn't hurt them to put them to sleep. Better safe, and all that; I've no objection to your being careful. Still, they do have remarkably stable reaction patterns. If either one were an ordinary transplant case, I'd have to write him, or her, up as bearing with the situation better than any previous transplants. Emotionally, that—"

"Him *or* her?" said the Tylervoice, with the husky overtones indicating Jailyn's presence. "Then . . . then it wasn't just a dream? I can actually talk to that . . . that man who . . . who had this body . . . oof. Doctor, one thing I insist on—some of you great medical brains are going to have to sit down seriously and invent a vocabulary to go along with these . . . states of consciousness, that won't make me feel like some kind of vampire or ghoul."

Dr Brian walked to the bed-hospital and smiled down at . . . *at Jailyn Rost*, he told himself, staring at the smooth young male face.

"Does it upset you emotionally to think of it that way?" he asked, making a few meaningless flourishes on the computer readout plate with his lightpen.

"Not really," she said, "but then, you're monitoring all the emotional reactions anyway, aren't you? So how can it really make a difference, what I think? I don't see how you can regard my opinions as to my subjective state as having any validity at all—at least, the way you must have me coked up."

Dr Brian shook has head. "Seriously, the major suppressants are used only in stress situations, and the monitor keeps us abreast of those. We've learned a lot, of course; compared to the others who have gone through transplants, you have sustained little or no panic reaction, after the first quite natural feelings of fear and revulsion . . . oh, certainly, there has been distress, occasionally considerable stress. But then, you're a tough-minded person, Miss Rost—as I'm sure I'm hardly the first to inform you!"

The Tylerface managed a slight smile. "I'm rich and I'm pigheaded—that's another way of putting it. Jimmy Tungo puts it that way all the time, but that's all right because he's rich and pigheaded too. Which, come to think of it . . . how is it I've had no visitors? I don't expect my family to show up, God knows—damn fool aunts and uncles are all I have left—but haven't there been *any* inquiries?"

"Do you realize how long it's been since the accident?" Dr Brian countered.

"Well . . . now that you mention it, I hadn't given it any thought, no, but I haven't been reading the newspapers lately, either, doctor."

Dr Brian nodded. "Over two months. Mr Tungo *was* here, for two straight weeks, but Transfed finally called obs on him—that's what he told me to tell you —and set him off on the *Gambit*. He was quite angry about it, and my assurances that he could not have hoped to talk to you for another two and a half months at a minimum hardly reconciled him."

"The *Gambit*? Then the *Miles High* must have—"

"Extensive repairs, I'm afraid. So they requisitioned Mr Tungo for the trans-Plutonian tests, since he couldn't even claim prior responsibility to the *Miles High*."

"Damned legalists. Transfed should—well, never mind. I'm more interested in . . . well, now, how do

I find words for this situation? . . . this body's previous tenant?" Tylerface grimaced faintly. "Who was he? What was he like? And . . . and how come I can talk to him in my head when it's *my* brains in here now, not his . . . doctor, *how much of me did you save?*"

Involuntarily Dr Brian shot a glance at Miss Kim, then looked down at the readout plate and judged that Jailyn was not seriously upset. That, of course, was one of the beauties of suppressants.

"What do *you* think about being a transplant subject?" he countered.

"Never mind what I think—oh, well, I suppose you won't tell me if I don't tell you. I think . . . *hell*, doctor, how should I know what I think at a time like this? You're the doctor and you imply I'm going to live; so, well . . . I'm alive and until I die I'll stay alive. I guess that's it. Hardly profound philosophy, I suppose.

"I mean, as long as I'm alive, well, I can make the most of whatever it is; I suppose it's going to be rough. It's got to be rough; goes with the territory." She attempted to shrug. "But I can make it if others have lived through it. Others have managed, I know. So—*I'll* manage.

"Even with a . . . man's body."

Dr Brian decided she wouldn't have been human if her voice hadn't weakened, cracked a tiny bit, toward the end of all those brave words.

The readout continued to confirm the fundamental stability of her mind while confronting the question.

"Very well," he said. "As you may have suspected, there *is* more to this case than I have so far felt free to tell you. And I tell you this early, partly because of your insistence."

"All right, all right," Jailyn broke in impatiently, "you don't need to apologize every time you tell me something—or don't. I'm a patient; I understand."

Dr Brian allowed himself to show a sneer for every

patient he'd ever had but Jailyn Rost. "Offhand, you're the first patient I've met who's ever said such a thing, at least to me."

"You've never had me for a patient before. Come on now, let's have it straight."

"You are right-handed, Miss Rost. In the accident, enough of the right half of your brain was destroyed to make it, uh, unsalvageable. But your left lobe, fortunately the dominant one, defining and containing the greater part of your memory, your skill, your personality, language arts, your left lobe was usable. Coming up in the future, of course, will be extensive and exhaustive—exhausting!—tests concerning just what you *have* lost. Inevitably some motor skills, memories, have been lost; some retraining may be indicated in some areas, though our monitoring has picked up nothing seriously wrong. On that count you may feel comforted—and, my dear Miss Rost, you may count yourself extremely fortunate."

Tylereyes stared solemnly at him, waiting.

"Now, then, your new body belonged to one Benjy Tyler, who was nineteen years old. He was, roughly speaking, mentally retarded beyond the capabilities of modern science, as we modern scientists put it." Dr Brian essayed a chuckle. It fell absolutely flat, and he resumed, a tinge of color on his cheeks that Jailyn did not miss.

"He was mentally retarded, but not physically. Perhaps it was a touch of some plaguewar modification of PK imbalance that slipped by the postpartum exams. Several weeks before your own unfortunate accident, he finally managed to fall on his head. His midbrain and cerebellum were undamaged, fortunately for you since yours were destroyed; they freezeboxed him and we began waiting for the inevitable accident to happen to someone who matched Benjy sufficiently to minimize the quantity of immune-reaction suppressants, altogether unpleasant substances to inflict on a body when not necessary. And his mother, after the accident, had finally given up and decided to let what was left of him be of some use to the world."

"I'd like to meet her."

Dr Brian shook his head immediately. "Perhaps, but I wouldn't try it. She never wants to see Benjy again —considers her son dead, even wrote him out of her will. Perhaps she could use some treatment, but she's not certifiable, unfortunately for you . . . well, at any rate, she was careful to inform me that the new possessor of her son's body could forget any claims of any nature against the Tyler estates. If it hadn't been for her real generosity in making Benjy's body available, I'd have to admit frankly that I found her a thoroughly unpleasant woman."

"Not at all," Jailyn said. "I understand her position completely, though it makes things both a little more and a little less awkward. Damn; I'd shrug if I could move my shoulders."

Dr Brian sat back and wondered if she would push for more information; he expected that she probably would.

"Now, then, doctor, you don't think you've fooled me into thinking you've told me all that's on your mind about my little problems, do you?"

"Hm, no," Dr Brian said, clearing his throat. "Well . . ."

I can't bring myself to say the words to her, he realized after a moment, amazed with himself.

Tylereyes gazed up at him.

There was silence in the room, ever-lengthening silence. . . .

"Come, come, doctor, I'm a big girl now." She chuckled. "A big boy, too, it seems. Now, I'm alive; so you can't scare me there. Does this body have some hideous terminal disease? Is that it? I can take it, doctor, I promise you. I'm aware I'm lucky to be as alive as I am."

"I'm glad you feel that way," said Dr Brian truthfully. "No, nothing . . . gloomy, not like that."

"Well, then," she said, impatient at last and feeling her temper, "what is it? You say Benjy's brain is gone and only half of mine is left—what did you do? Did you have to put someone else's half-brain in here with me, or something? Come on, tell me what's . . ."

Tylereyes widened to see color draining from Dr Jon Brian's face.

There was another silence, brief this time; but subjectively interminable.

"You are . . . a remarkably astute woman, Miss Rost. Host bodies, as you no doubt are aware, are rare in the extreme, due to the hideous complexity of legalities that now surround the whole transplant topic. It was . . . only a few days after your own accident, while we were already preparing the Benjybody for your operation, that we heard of another accident remarkably similar to yours—oh, not a spacedrive burning out; the fellow was some kind of technician on the new multiwave asteroid project; an asteroid jockey. The outside antenna of the multiwave generator spectacularly malfunctioned while he was out there with it, investigating.

"Miss Rost, he was by an incredible cross-coincidence left-handed, and the left side of his head was, well, injured beyond recovery. Considering he was also a reasonable type-match for Benjy . . . you take my meaning; it was an opportunity we could not pass up. Opposite *and* dominant lobes surviving . . . putting them in the one body . . . it was the only way to save both of you, all three if you count Benjy. I won't go into the gains for scientific knowledge. By the way, our readout analyses are leading to the rather unusual conclusion that a noticeable amount of personality residue is present in Benjy's surviving midbrain and cerebellum. Another new variable factor we had not anticipated, but . . ."

"So . . ." Jailyn whispered, "so . . . *three* of us . . . and I suppose I should be horrified. But you've got all those suppressants handy; I hardly feel anything, just . . . curious, and . . . and just a little bit of, well, utter revulsion. In case I start deciding to go into screaming hysterics, though, you'd better—"

"Are you really the type?" smiled Dr Brian, over some inner uneasiness; the readout showed indications now of serious strains on some levels of Jailyn's personality. "Perhaps I should spend a bit more time emphasizing your relative good luck. The fact of the matter is that we have many more occasions in which we would *like* to try a brain transplant—hundreds a year, in fact. But we're lucky if we can find an appropriate host body, lucky indeed.

"You'd be surprised what a small percentage of those few host bodies made available are actually suitable, usable. Age is one factor; over forty, the host, that is, and the transplant simply doesn't work out. The body's in old ways, apparently, by that age.

"Others made available turn out to be terminal-illness cases, or with otherwise short life expectancies. The transplanting of an otherwise healthy brain into such a body is only a cruelly temporary prolongation of life. Then—"

"Doctor," Jailyn said wanly, "you've made your point. Could we touch on that little matter of who's sitting up here beside me these days?"

"Joe Winslow, multiwave technician, age twenty-seven, Leo male—"

Thin Tylersmile. "You researched my interests! Two Leos in the same body . . . well, it should be interesting. And Benjy?"

"Er, hm, hadn't thought . . ." Dr Brian scribbled a request for Benjy's birth date, and the readout plate winked back. "Capricorn. Is that significant? Not my field, you understand." He forbore another attempt at a chuckle.

A Tyler chuckle. "Some fun!"

"Miss Rost," interposed the nurse, "I've often wondered—how can you tell what sign they're born under
when people are born on Mars, or any of the offworld
settlements?"

"Now you've proved I'm only an amateur," Jailyn
said. "I never gave it thought, frankly. In the—in *this*
solar system, I should imagine that it's all the same
zodiac, no matter where you are. I don't really know.
But when we get interstellar travel, I don't think *any*-
one will know."

"*If* we get interstellar travel," said Dr Brian.

"Well, yes. I don't think it's very likely, myself. But,
now, as long as I'm still nice and cheerful from all the
guck in my system—tell me more about this Winslow.
It must have been him, not the Tyler boy, I was . . .
dreaming . . . with, last night."

"Well, I could give you his life history as we know
it, but we can't really say we have him all down on
paper. Professionally speaking, I really think you two
ought to, hm, er, get to know each other without any
prejudicially superficial facts from me."

"Does he know? You know, it seems like madness,
pure madness, lying here and discussing these things so
calmly, but . . ."

"No, he doesn't. We decided, or I decided, you were
the more inherently stable—and I might add your response has borne out my expectation splendidly. You
must not think that our repertoire of chemical suppressants and electronic monitoring is an automatic,
full, or complete barrier between you and the possibility of insanity. That would be a kind of insanity in
itself. The fact that you are able to look calmly upon
what has occurred to you is as much a tribute to your
own mind as it is to science."

"Doctor, I may not be so much the ideal patient
once it really starts sinking in; mostly I feel as if I'm
only in shock, deep in shock, insulated. It's as if it

doesn't really mean anything to *me*. And I know that's not true, so . . . Not only that, I can see where we are going to have a lot of problems I'll just bet you never stopped to think of—"

"Don't be too sure," Dr Brian said. "There have been a lot of transplants, and our records are voluminous. We have an extensive library of data on which to base our rehabilitation program—which in a sense you have already embarked upon."

"I suppose that's a comfort," Jailyn said dryly. "Are you diddling with those dials to make me sleepy again? That's really not very polite of you."

"Now, now," said Dr Brian, "you will get quickly tired for quite some weeks yet; I hope you won't accuse us every time it happens! I promise you, I won't use suppressants unless readout indicates clearly a level of stress beyond my estimate of your strength at the time."

"Then I'm just getting naturally tired?"

"That's correct. Ah, it's not precisely correct to say I will use suppressants only in danger situations. I shall have to bring up Mr Winslow from time to time; and I intend to have only one of you up at a given time. I have at present no solid ideas on how you two would both be able to communicate with me, if you were simultaneously awake—and I think it could be highly difficult for you also.

"That's the basic plan, too, as you may know—our basic system is to let transplantees sleep, and dream, as much as possible. We don't know the mechanism, but it seems to make the period of adjustment much easier. You understand, we were not precisely in a position to ask permission when the decision was made to go ahead with this, hm, project."

"Very well," Jailyn said. "Then I think I'll just drop off naturally, then; or as naturally as pos

". . . found ourselves placed in a peculiar position shortly after an accident you yourself may even have

heard about, before your own. An ion-drive breakdown
on the experimental ship *Miles High*, it was, almost
killing Jailyn Rost."

Tylerface frowned with Joe Winslow's suddenly tense
mind. "Sure, I remember that—heard about it, oh,
maybe half an hour before I went out cleaning Monstro's ears. . . . Jailyn Rost, space pioneer, eh? A con-
federationist, too—anti-Paulsted. Well, but what the
hell, it was a rotten way to go, for a woman or anyone.
What's it have to do with me?"

"You'll recall saying you were 'good and braced for
anything,' a few minutes back?"

"Get *on* with it, doc," said Winslow impatiently.

"Yes," said Dr Brian, nettled in spite of himself at
the man's not too unconsciously arrogant tone. Al Zink,
that supervisor of Winslow's from Transfed, had been
the same way—they were as bound up in their damned
multiwave as Paulsted, or . . .

Dr Brian smiled to himself then at his weakness, for
he was just as bound up in his brain transplants. . . .

"Well, then," Dr Brian said, checking the readout
more carefully than might have appeared from his
casual glances, "you lost the left lobe of your cerebrum,
and all of your midbrain and cerebrum—enough to
make salvage impossible, at any rate. As a left-handed
man with a probably dominant right lobe, however,
you are at a minimum perhaps 75 percent intact—
memories, personality, etc. Unfortunately motor capabilities involve the missing lower portions of your brain,
but your host body is providing that, so physical retraining along those lines won't be too arduous.

"In case you're wondering at your own calm, the
drugs in your system are very effective; and later, when
the drugs are no longer being used, you should be quite
accustomed to the situation.

"You're quite fortunate, actually. Since the glial cells
tend to cross-file memory informations that validate

the personality, the identity, in both lobes, you may end up with only a 5 or 10 percent total loss. You could, after all, have lost three-quarters of your personality had the multiwave blast, or whatever it was, hit part of your right cerebral lobe as well."

"Doctor, I appreciate this rather weird and frightening rundown on how I have and haven't lost my real self, and all. But in case you're wondering why you aren't picking up more anxiety on your readout there, I happen to have some practical knowledge of brain-damage theory. A cousin of mine was studying the field, and got killed in a freak lab accident when I was a kid. I took it up for a while, you know, like a kid will, carrying the torch onward, as it was. Uh, well, the cousin, she was a girl, you know—older than me, and everything. Well . . . I had a crush on her. It hit me pretty hard when she was killed. Got me interested in her field so maybe something could be done about such things—this was all before the first successful brain transplant, you understand.

"But I got bored after a while; it wasn't really my kind of interest. Then the multiwave generators were perfected, and that, well, that's been all I've been interested in since then. Say, I do run on a lot at the mouth, don't I, doc?"

"Because, for all your impatience, you don't really want to hear what I'm telling you," Dr Brian said, deliberately.

Tylereyes looked reproachfully up at him, but Winslow couldn't find anything to say in response.

Anxiety was definitely showing up now on his readout, serious anxiety. Part of it could be traced to Winslow's compulsive exposition of his memories, but the rest . . .

Dr Brian decided to get on with it.

"I'm going to tell you anyway, because you're too intellectualized—you'll just get your mind tied into solipsist knots, for all our druggings, and that could make a problem for us.

"Jailyn Rost is right-handed—as in fact Benjy Tyler was, or is, though with him it hardly mattered. Her left lobe survived unimpaired; we could have saved a small portion of the visual centers of her right lobe, but it hardly seemed feasible, especially after your accident came to our attention.

"Benjy Tyler was the first and only host body suitable for either of you, and you and Jailyn Rost were the only two suitable transplants around for the Tyler body.

"And so I believe you've already met Miss Rost—in your dreams."

Tylereyes closed. "So that's the champagne, and the dancing on the lawn under cold clear stars till dawn came up, and the—you mean I'm *sharing my* brain *with somebody else?*"

"Tch, tch, Mr Winslow," Dr Brian said, a wry smile on his face, "I expected clearer thinking of you. The Benjy-body has half of her cerebrum, half of yours, in both cases the half that survived in salvageable condition. Pardon my emphasis on the words 'salvageable,' for you would both be dead now if it weren't for the Tyler body *and* scientific progress in the last ten years."

"What the hell gave you the idea you could play God like this?"

"God?" Dr Brian sneered. "I thought he died a hundred years ago—and was buried under the plaguewar corpses."

"Damn the plaguewars. What gave you the idea—"

"You enjoy the thought of being dead now?"

"Shit, no, who would?"

"Well, then, stop yammering like a baby who's had its all-day sucker taken away. We gave you another one back, and just because you've got to share it, for that matter with a girl who has taken the whole thing a hell of a lot better than you have—"

"You've got your damn nerve talking to a patient like that," Winslow said indignantly.

"Now, stop your grandstanding, Winslow; I can practically read your mind, and I'm sure you're fully aware of the fact. All this is just slowing us down—or haven't you realized the job that's still ahead of you? Of course you have, and it fascinates you, too. Your subconscious has been churning out new hypotheses to test at a fantastic rate. In fact, this whole thing strikes you more as a challenge than as anything else, doesn't it?"

Tylereyes closed, then opened, staring coldly at Dr Brian.

"You are manipulating me, you bastard, cut it out. Can't you leave me *some* privacy? After all—"

"Privacy? You'll have to earn it, Winslow. First, there'll be monitoring of all three of you till we're certain your new body's being run right. Then, after that, there's advanced coordination exercises, physical and mental. There'll be—"

"All right, all right, for a moment. But how about chewing on these hypotheses: One, what if we *can't* function together? Which of us do you get rid of? Two, what about if *we* feel we're doing ok, and *you* figure we need another five years' close observation."

Winslow stopped and savored the next few sentences before saying anything. He had taken a solid dislike to Dr Brian, he decided; time to twist the knife.

"Now, then, I don't think you realize the implications of my old interest in the field—I heard all about Boardman's hidden labs, and those twenty-seven experiments that never got published anywhere. Ho. Your face pales. You too have heard of them. Interesting. Well, you've got some proving to do to *me*. This Jailyn Rost, what she knows or can do, I don't know anything about that, but I'm stuck with her, ho, ho. But as for you, I trust you when you prove I can."

"Well, now, that's unfortunate." Dr Brian struggled

to calm himself; what had possessed him to lose his temper at this stage? Part of it was simulated temper, of course, but the man *had* irritated him. "I seem to have overstimulated you; my sole intention was to arouse your interest in life," he began.

"Sure," Winslow said. "I believe you."

They exchanged chilly smiles.

"Mr. Winslow, both you and Miss Rost are, fortunately, natural optimists; your records indicate tone-scale variations dipping below the line so rarely as to be extremely significant when they do. If I were to tell you now how far below the line you were half an hour ago, you would flatly not believe me."

"How much Chinese blood have you got, doctor? You're too subtle for me. I said you're going to have to level with me, and I meant it. I'm going to need information, and lots of it. I know nothing of psychology, and nothing of female psychology—in spite of years of field studies." He broke off to laugh at that, but found he didn't really want to. "And I know little enough about what's happened in this whole transplant field in the last ten years. Information, doc, and lots of it. That's how *I'm* going to spend my time."

"I'm quite agreeable to letting you spend a portion of your waking time in study, Mr Winslow, in return for cooperation with me during another portion, and a third portion of cooperation with Miss Rost."

Tylereye winked at the doctor, without humor. "You can't fool me—you'll give me as little free time as possible. That can be worked out. I'm willing to go along with you for . . . well, how long will it take Miss Rost and me to . . . to do whatever it is we'll have to do in order to survive?"

"Believe me, Mr Winslow, I don't know, and I can't know until we've done it. Six months, say, at the utmost—but you might make it in six days or six hours. There are aspects of the mind's capabilities about which we can predict nothing, nothing whatsoever. And Boardman's notes were lost when the place was K-bombed by the deaders, so what we could have gleaned from his bizzarre experiments about unusual side effects now has to be learned over from scratch, and in far more orthodox fashion." Carefully he kept himself from sounding regretful.

"So. It *was* the deaders that did it, eh? I've always wondered about that—thanks for the free info, doc; I guess I'll give you some more voluntary cooperation in exchange. Keep the universe in balance, and all."

Dr Brian bit his lip, but said, "Very well. I'd sooner I'd said nothing rather than let that slip, but you seemed so well up on the subject that . . . no matter."

"You don't mind your nurse knowing? *I* don't give a damn, it's all ancient history, but—"

Nurse Kim adjusted the computer monitor, and came to the bed-hospital. "Boardman's assistant was a Korean genius who happened to be my stepfather. I may possibly know more about some of the . . . bizarre aspects, than Dr Brian here."

"My dear," Dr Brian said, turning to her, "you never cease to amaze me. No wonder you wanted this job." He turned back to the Tylerbody. "As for your wanting to know about your, er, partner, I'm not so sure I envy you sharing a body with that much of a woman. Your one advantage is that the male glands in your new body will be on your side; on the other hand, the blood to her brain has certain synthetic female hormones added to it, for her sanity's sake, so . . ."

"You make it sound like warfare, doc. Is that your real prognosis?"

"It wasn't till I began integrating certain aspects of this charming little talk we've been having."

Tylerbody sighed. "Apparently you've already begun picking Miss Rost's mind."

"Oh, yes," Dr Brian agreed, cheerfully. "Both of

you—all the time! But your conscious personalities are important too."

"Huh. Prognosis, doc, if you don't mind."

"It's within the parameters of possibility you two may be unable to stand each other, though the indications run against such a conclusion. If you do have basic conflict, you'll probably never be able to establish direct communication, mind to mind. You understand this is a new situation, in effect. . . ."

"Boardman, yes. Maybe the deaders were a little overeager."

"Too late now for regret." Dr Brian stopped himself from saying more.

"Aren't you a little afraid we may end up with the secret power to cloud men's minds so they cannot see us, or something? I mean, what if we get the power to take over the world, or you, or . . . or something?"

"Or something. Yes. Well, the human brain does use electricity and does generate an electric field. It is slight enough, however, that I have no plans for interrupting my sleep with making plans against such contingencies."

"Oh, well, I never wanted to be a Secret Master anyway."

"That's fine, Mr Winslow. Now I would say it is about time for you to go off to sleep and renew your acquaintance with Miss Rost."

"And Benjy—that's weird, like having a huge inarticulate puppy of a man tucked way in the back of my head. What's he still doing around, without a brain?"

"All he lacks are the two cerebral hemispheres you and Miss Rost have so generously contributed to him. Personality does not entirely reside in the cerebrum; you as a student of such matters should have been aware of that."

"Aware is one thing. Experiencing it is another."

"Time to sleep, Mr Winslow. You'll learn far more,

I assure you." Dr Brian nodded to Miss Kim, who began moving dials.

"How does that stuff work?" Winslow asked, futilely trying to raise his head to follow the nurse's actions. "Does it drop me off sharply? Or does it just taper off gent

CHAPTER SIX

When I was a young lad courting the girls . . .
say, I haven't had a good dirty dream in so long I'm
beginning to wonder if—

I'd really rather you didn't.

Hi, there. What's a nice girl like you—

*Stop that. It's hard to take jokes about this. Just like
those dreams of yours. Every time you start, it begins
triggering certain . . . er . . . memories that, well,
that are mine, and I don't want you dreaming my love
life, thank you.*

Sounds like fun! How can I persuade you to
change your mind?

Can't.

Come on, now, we're supposed to cooperate; I
want a good dirty dream and you tell me you keep
canceling them. Say, how do you manage it, anyway?

Oh, I've been talking to Benjy. Benjy listens to me.

BENJY LIKES JJ

Jesus! Was that him? Felt almost like real words
that time.

*He learns fast; yes, that was Benjy. You should pay
more attention to him, you'd learn a lot.*

First off, I'd still like to know how come he's still

around in the first place. As a personality, I mean. I mean, we're here now!

First, he didn't have that much personality. Second, all transplantees have insisted that they've felt some personality residue from the host body.

You been talkin' to the doc behind my back again.

No, that's just what he was telling you, only you weren't listening closely enough. Well, he did give me a medical text on the subject, a popularization.

How come I don't get to read it too?

So read it. It's still in the service rack, I'm sure. It asimovs the subject pretty well.

Ok, ok, I don't have time to read everything—especially when I don't get that much time to. Exercise, exercise! I always hated it in the first place. Listen, "personality residue" was way after my time."

Just think of it basically as a sense of Benjy's "I-ness" surviving, and remember that there do seem to be orders of memory in the cerebellum and even in the midbrain. It's where a lot of our habits come from, in a sense—that's why we're a little extra-lucky, since Benjy never bothered himself with a lot of complex and worrisome body habits.

Habits? Sure, but—

You don't realize how much your habits are you, or rather how much of your time they take. For instance, one thing's sure—we have to learn how to get along together, and you're not spending enough time at that.

Are you trying to give me orders too? And anyway, aren't we asleep? How come this is making so much sense?

We are asleep; but we're only using a tiny fraction of our attention on this. If you and I both stopped thinking this way at each other and started listening, we'd be right there dreaming. Mostly we are already, only this little part of us doesn't quite realize it.

Whew! There's a dilly of a theory. But if we're mostly dreaming, who's doing the thinking, here?

You call this thinking?

Well, conversing, anyway. Doesn't that take coordination of lots of various—

A small tap into the speech centers. Like a leaky faucet. I used to wake up when I was in my teens, and run my dreams for a little while, a lot like this. Funny, I just remembered that. Anyway, we're consciously verbalizing at each other now; I imagine that when we . . . graduate, we'll just be sort of in tune with each other. Maybe a lot of the time we won't even have to use words. It's an old philosophical question, you know —do you need language in order to think?

For being sound asleep you're a pretty wordy woman, lady.

Smile when you say that, sleepyhead!

I don't know whether we're making progress or not, but I just realized we got clean away from what I was thinking about. This sex business, why, there's aspects—*uh!*—what did you *do?*

Quit it. We're not ready yet; give us a while.

Winslow withdrew suddenly from the odd give-and-take he couldn't be sure was conversation, dream, or nightmare; and with the withdrawal he was plunged into a void of blueness and then into a costumed swaggerer of the Aughts, the wild decade between 2000 and 2010 C.E. that brought the Western world ultimately back part-way from the Changes of the eighties

Beside him in the great geodesic dome that was the great meeting hall of the Confederation of the Post-Colonies stood a tall young beautiful girl with dark brown hair, her body hidden under many swaths of translucent thin green fabrics from mutated postplague-war silkworms.

He bowed to her; she graciously inclined her head at him, then waved one long thin hand.

From it sprang a tiny figure that immediately expanded into a full-sized replica of the girl. The replica immediately raised one hand, from which sprang another tiny replica which immediately expanded, gestured, and multiplied thus onward till Winslow in his bright red garb was surrounded by thirteen identical Jailyns in green swaths of delicate light shimmering, and they said as one, "And you wished to discourse of love? What do you know of it? Until you understand, or till you wish to, farewell!"

The thirteen vanished instantly, and then the great dome, and he was plunged back into blueness, and then was aware of the presence of Jailyn's brooding thought near him—silent.

. . .

Uh. Damn, it's quiet!

. . .

Uh.

. . .

All I want is a little tiny orgy scene. Why, when we get out of this place, I'm going to get us into one of the biggest real-life orgies you ever heard of! And believe me, I know just the people who can help out! Hey! Where are you?

. . .

Hey, no fair shutting up like that. You don't understand.

. . .

I mean, can't you be philosophic about it? *Hey!*

. . .

It can't just be prudishness.

. . .

Sigh.

. . .

Ok, come back here. You can't . . . can't just leave me alone like this! I . . . I can't take it! But you gotta understand, too.

. . .

Benjy. Benjy, are you there?

BENJY SAY DON'T FIGHT.

I don't want to fight. Make her talk!

BENJY SAY DON'T FIGHT. DON'T HURT. DON'T BE HURT. BENJYSAYJOEDON'TFIGHT.

Are you ready to listen a little bit, Joe?

Uh, well, sure, I guess so. If—

No "ifs," but if you mean you want me to understand that you're going to be thinking things like that because it's your nature to, then I understand.

Oh. Oh, well . . .

And perhaps if you're beginning to catch on, you're willing to listen?

Lay on, Lady Macduff!

This isn't really a laughing matter we're in now.

You know, I have the funniest feeling I'm dreaming about the rings of Saturn, or is that Sauron, or—

I am Jailyn Rost, or a small portion of her sleeping mind that is, along with a portion of yours, ignoring carefully a vast and intricate dream I am at present dreaming about the rings of Saturn, which—

First off, I can see our saga is *not* going to be one of the epic love stories. But I'm with you.

Now shut up and listen, if you're going to learn anything. We've got to be mixing dreams—dreams at the least!—from now until one or more of us winks out for good, so we might as well get used to it. Now, we're dreaming that we're talking about dreaming while we're talking and dreaming and . . .

Ok, that's clear enough.

But he made his mind shut up, after the one sarcastic shot, and

it was the *Miles High* and it was quite a little bit of Monstro also; and in another sense the whole thing was only Benjy, which was puzzling but seemed inescapably true. It was also simply a vast lounge with transparent walls extrapolated from Monstro and the *Miles High* viewing rooms. Glasses clinked at the proper punctuating moments at low conversations mumbling on at nearby tables, dim-seen through billows of Venusian cave incense.

Out past the viewscreens or simply transparent walls Winslow could feel the presence of the multiwave generators, throbbing incomprehensibly in their necklace orbit round the sun.

Jailyn sat opposite him at the small emerald table. She was swathed again from neck to foot in yards and yards of soft fabric this time with an impossibly metallic sheen of diamond-silver alloy.

Winslow could not perceive her figure at all through this material, which nettled him; immediately he realized he was clad only in a Marsminer's breechclout. Instead of the dozens of submicrotools he'd grown used to, that summer he'd spent in Marsmine Twenty-five, there were a myriad tiny jewels, each of which glittered with impossible inner fires.

"Mercurian sundrops," Jailyn said, observing his puzzled frown. "Pretty, yes?"

"Oh, yes," Winslow agreed. "Of course, they don't exist at temperatures below 5,000° Standard, but I won't argue."

"Good," said Jailyn, nodding her head satisfiedly.

Winslow banished traces of sleepiness from his mind, observing her features carefully, without caring that it was obvious he was doing so. Undoubtedly she was quite an attractive girl—but she seemed not to have a controlled self-image, a part of him whispered with a certain secret satisfaction. Otherwise she would not *shift* that way. . . .

"You are quite correct, Mr Winslow," Jailyn said. "Few people have a truly steady self-image of themselves. You yourself, though obviously a rather handsome man in a somewhat crude way, are not at all certain what you look like to others. Fortunately it

hardly makes a difference when we're . . . awake,
since we'll never see our real faces again except in old
solidos."

Winslow was nettled. It seemed like an old argument
they'd been having for years. "Do you have to keep
harping on that?" It was much more pleasant to observe what shifted and settled and moved and rested
in the field of vision that was his mind perceiving
this. . . .

"My, my," she smiled. "It's as if we'd been married
for years and years and years, isn't it? But *I* would say
we're in another kind of prison than marriage—and
we're bound in by the good Dr Brian."

Winslow squinted, once more irritated, but determined to hear her out.

"*He* wants us to learn to get along together, and
we're not going to get to do any other single thing we
might *really* want to do until then. If then."

"Such as walk out of this hospital, or spaceship.
. . ." He felt a swirl of disorientation. "Of course, we
don't need the ship, do we?"

Jailyn smiled at him. "No?"

"Nonsense, of course not. We could as well be out
there between the rings and the surface. Besides, you
think I don't know about space? You forget I'm a multiwave man—space may be a dream, an impracticality,
but it's mine just as much as yours. Come on, let's
go on out!"

There did not seem ever to have been a *Miles High*-
Monstro mutation. The velvet eternity of space was
slashed by the curved nested knives of Saturn's rings
on one side of them, and by the monstrous stormy-
clouded surface of squat Saturn himself on the other.

". . . go on out of the hospital, as I was saying, and
do anything we want. My dear Lady Jailyn, I twigged
the good doctor too. Right out of the original Fred
Boardman mold. Some of it's got to be necessary to

us, but I'll bet you solits to oldbucks he's programed things for us to do till the latter seventies!"

"Exactly. I'm gratified to see you grasping our position so clearly. Quite frankly, I'm not in the least a stupid woman, nor once you skip the ego games are you a stupid man. Of course, we all have our ego games, but that's part of the problem."

"Do you have any idea of what we're up against? Jailyn, we can try to . . . to merge our minds, or whatever the program's to be—but what if we lose our minds, fracture completely, go out and not come back, lose our identities, crazy, you know? Like that idea? Go for that?" Winslow frowned to himself. He hardly felt he cared any longer; why was he going on like this?

"Lose our—"

Jailyn broke off and studied Winslow as the two of them hung motionless in space, Saturn immense on one side, his rings incredible on the other; slabs, sheets, and torrents of stars everywhere else in the impossible unreachable distance.

She tried a different direction. "How much do you know about identity, anyway?"

"Like the countryfolk say, I guess—I don't know what I see when the lights go out, but I know it's mine."

"Well . . . you're going to have to do better than that. I don't care about countryfolk wasting their lives doing whatever stupid things they rot their existence with. I just know I've been realizing things lately. I guess we've been mostly dreaming for months. Maybe this is the first time we've really noticed *what* we've been dreaming about. At least, it seems certain to me there's a sense in which we'll lose our identities, no doubt, and another in which we won't."

"How come you have this all figured out already?"

She ignored the sarcasm. "Do you know, I'm not sure

at all? Mostly I'll bet it has something to do with the
suppressants—we've mostly been living in semicom-
plete sensory deprivation while we've not been exercising and taking the good doctor's tests. Rest, sleep,
dream—the mind is left free to think unimpeded by
having to mind the body-store, free to concentrate, to
clarify.

"Besides, everything in this body's Benjy's, right up
through the spinal cord to the medulla, the pons, the
whole midbrain, the cerebellum; I don't *need* to mind
the store.

"My mind is all they left me, and you—and Benjy
and the bed-hospital—are taking care of about 98 percent of what has to be done. My mind . . . and
time to use it. Or am I sleeping? Not working at
all?"

He watched her mouth close, become kissable—he
pinched off that thought quickly, instinctively. Her
brow furrowed and for a second he thought she had become angry at the flash of desire. But she had not
noticed.

Winslow allowed his body to rotate slightly with
several relative vectors simultaneously, so that the
rings, the stars, Saturn, the rings, the stars, Saturn,
drifted by over and over again in complex nonrepeti-
tive patterns that he did not so much notice as *become.* . . .

"Aren't we maybe being far too verbal about all
this?" He found himself talking with a sense of astonishment deep within him, for he had not thought he
had willed himself to communicate, nor had he thought
he had anything to communicate at that moment.

Jailyn smiled, and Winslow saw it even though at the
time his eyes were sweeping along with a dust storm on
Saturn's surface, a storm 20,000 miles long, or was it
dust?

"Of course we're too verbal," she said. "And that's

probably a part of the problem we'll never completely solve."

"Why?"

"Dr Brian. He wants verbalizations—whether he knows it or not. Though it's not that simple. If we tell him we're getting along fine, that's a verbalization, but he's going to want to know *how* we're 'getting along fine.'"

"Say, how are we ever going to catch any real sleep if we go around all the time gabbing along like this?"

"Did you forget? This is a dream right now—where's your space helmet?"

"Yeah, uh . . . ok. But it just doesn't seem so . . . so restful, you know, zipping around solving problems like this all the time, or trying to, at least. And—"

"What do you think dreaming is?"

"Are you kidding? Simple—cleaning out the computer banks, erasing old memory chains that aren't needed any more, sorting out the day's impressions to see which ones to keep, that sort of thing. Working out the traumas of the days, engrammatic incidents, problems—oh."

He said the "oh" in a fairly low voice, and his face puckered up as though he were going to whistle noncommittally.

She nodded. "Problem solving. And would you say we've got some problems to solve? Your answer is yes? Fine. Now here's some answers from me.

"First, as to that sex question that was exercising you so much, a short time back. That's mostly my problem, and it's a big one; I'll admit that. I'll even admit I've been having some of the strangest, most hung-up . . . lesbian-type dreams you can imagine, which is a thing I never did before. I mean, I was always well-adjusted to my sexuality, and . . . and, well, I said it before. It's my problem.

"You, all you have to do is learn how to . . . how

to get along with a set of tools that may not be cali-
brated quite the same as your old ones, but which
are made for the same . . . the same process. Me, I'm
going to have to . . . to . . . well, I don't know *what*
I'm going to have to do. I don't like any of the even-
tualities I can extrapolate.

"But I'm going to have to keep all my ideas, theories,
dreams, fears, expectations . . . all that strictly to myself until I do work it out for myself, as much as possible. If that makes you feel left out, I'm sorry; we're
in this together, God knows, but this particular problem's all mine."

She actually smiled at him, and it was a cheerful
smile. Weak, but definitely cheerful. It made him feel
a little better for the first time.

Then a jumble of reactions hit him. "What about
later. Yes, when we do get out, and damned if I'll let
them keep me—us—in this bed a minute longer than
we have to . . . and, well, you know, this *is* a healthy
male body. I suppose I could take pills to suppress . . .
well, you know . . . but then, I'd still be a prisoner in
a way, wouldn't I? And Benjy too, for that matter,
though I don't suppose he'd know what he's been missing—"

"I told you you should have gotten to know him
sooner!" Jailyn's tone was suddenly, inexplicably,
mischievous. "His mother never found out about a
certain maid who used to make regular trips to Benjy's
bed when he was still at home and—hold your breath—
fourteen. He seems to have enjoyed it a lot, but it never
impressed him strongly enough to make him go out
and do something stupid about it, like trying to rape
his sister, or something—not that his parents had any
other children, after the way he turned out. Such
being the cruel practicality of our times . . ."

"The kid's sterile, of course," said Winslow. The law
would have left no alternative.

"Tie-off only, though. Damned if his mother hadn't thought unselfishly about a transplant even back then before transplants. And if it could be proved Benjy's . . . condition wasn't congenital, then the law couldn't say anything. But that seems pretty insignificant right now."

"Sorta nice to know, though. I wonder what kind of children the three of us would manage to father?"

It rather astonished Winslow, but Jailyn laughed. "He'd have some father-image hangups!"

Winslow grinned. "Perhaps that's the missing ingredient—a sense of humor! We make it through this thing after all!"

"That reminds me—one thing we haven't considered. I don't think we necessarily have to tell the good doctor *everything* we learn."

"Yes, as long as we don't give him the idea we're holding things back."

"Right," said Jailyn.

"Then let's shake on it!" Winslow stuck out his hand—and saw the rings of Saturn through it. A bolt of fear jabbed through him.

"*What's the matter!*" Jailyn's whisper was filled with urgent distress.

"I . . . I can see through me!"

She closed her eyes, and giggled. She placed her hands in front of her face and looked at him through the fingers. "This is a dream, Joe Winslow, remember? Don't worry about what you see or don't see, it doesn't mean a thing."

A brilliant dot he felt as a warmth, like the multi-wave generators, detached itself from the rings and began to speed toward the two of them. Larger and brighter it got; an asteroid.

She pointed at it. "Take that asteroid, for instance. I brought it over because I thought you should see—"

"But it's Monstro!"

"Oh?"

The asteroid hovered next to them, shattered multi-wave-generator ear scattered over its surface, an open airlock just beyond.

"Say," Winslow said, "I'd just as soon wake up from this dream, you know? I don't really think I'm up to all this changing about, after all!"

"But it's only illusion, Joe, you shouldn't—I tell you, have you ever been to Mars?"

Winslow looked at her.

She shimmered then, became transparent.

"Don't *do* that," he said, alarmed. "Even dreaming, it's most unsettling!"

"I was about to take us to my lovely castle on Mars," Jailyn said, her voice getting fainter, "but it seems the good doctor is waking me up. Sleep tight, and don't worry! I'll be back in a while! Play around and have fun!"

And she vanished.

Immediately the rings of Saturn, the stars, Saturn itself, vanished also, and for a brief moment Joe Winslow drifted, his senses completely inoperative.

No.

He concentrated on Jailyn, held on to the thought of the girlform of her, swathed in yards of gleaming cloth, tried to remember the saucy tilt of her nose and the wicked humor in her eyes and the color, the color of them, was it blue deep as Earth seas from synchronorbit . . .

. . . and there she was, no, not as in the dream, but her, indefinably, awake, up, up, up theretheretherethere-awakefaraway . . . and she was talking and listening and talking awake and he was asleep and it was so hard sooo haaard soooooooooooooo haaaaaaaaaaaaaaaa rrrrrrddddddddd—uh—to follow, wanna jus sleepsleep sleep

Hey. Hey, yeah! Benjy! Hey, Benjy, where are you?

. . .

Funny, no one there. Maybe I'm too wakey instead of sleepy . . . but I'm sleepy too . . . funny, sleep, wake, I should be scared, all uncertainty and ohhhhh

hhhhhhh, deeper, thatttttt'ssss ittttt . . . Can't be up there listening to her talk to the doctor and still talk to Benjy wherever he is down there cerebellum how do you talk to a cerebellum you've never been properly introduced to . . . Benjy?

BENJY LISTEN. ALL THE TIME. BENJY LIKE FLYING BY PRETTY LIGHTS. YOU GO NICE PLACES, TAKE ME ALONG. HAPPY. HAPPYHAPPYHAPPY.

(You know, Benjy, I almost don't believe you're so easy to please, but—)

BENJY SAY TO BE HAPPY TOO. YOU DON'T KNOW. YOU ARE HAPPY BUT YOU DON'T KNOW IT. ONLY DIFFERENCE. BENJY HAPPY. EVERYBODY HAPPY. ONLY NOT EVERYBODY KNOW. I CAN TELL. BENJY TELLS.

Whew! Hey, that was only a parenthetical remark. I didn't—well, I don't suppose you know a parenthetical—

BENJY KNOWS WHEN YOU KNOW. BENJY FORGET SOON, BUT REMEMBERS WHEN YOU REMEMBER, KNOWS WHEN YOU KNOW. WHILE YOU KNOW. BENJY SMART WHEN YOU SMART. BUT YOU DON'T LISTEN WHEN BENJY IS SMART. YOU SAY EVERY DAY BENJY IS STUPID TODAY.

Uh, let me think about that one. Never occurred to me. Wasn't trying to put you down, Benjy, I like you too—we're all in this together, after all!

BENJY REMEMBER. SOMEBODY SAID THAT ONCE BEFORE. MAYBE MANY TIMES. BENJY PICKING UP BEING SMART. FUN, TOO.

Benjy, you're too much! You know, I'll bet, being in a bed-hospital like this, wired for just about everything, maybe you're getting smart because you don't have to run the body that much either, except when we're up and exercising.

BENJY NOT KNOW. NOT DO MUCH BEFORE, BENJY NOT
DO MUCH NOW. BENJY LISTEN BEFORE, NOT KNOW. BENJY
LISTEN NOW, NOT KNOW, BUT KNOW MAYBE LITTLE BIT
MORE. KNOW A LOT WHEN YOU TALK TO ME A LOT. KNOW
WORDS THEN. KNOW THOUGHTS THEN. YOU KNOW BENJY
WHAT HE MEAN?

Damned if I don't, after all. I don't understand,
but I believe.

BENJY NOT KNOW MUCH. BENJY KNOW MORE WHEN
YOU TAKE BENJY ALONG. BENJY HEAR YOU WANT JAY
BUT JAY WAKE UP AND TALK TO DOCTOR. JAY TOO FAR
FROM YOU, ME NOW. BENJY TOO FAR FROM YOU BEFORE
NOWNESS. YOU GO UP TO JAY, BENJY TOO FAR AGAIN.
YOU TEACH, LEARN, BENJY TO COME UP WITH YOU AND
JAY. ALL HAPPY TOGETHER THEN.

I dunno . . .

DOCTOR WANT SOME GOOD THINGS, SOME BAD THINGS.
BENJY HELP DO GOOD. BENJY NEVER HELP DO BAD.

And you tell the difference how?

BENJY KNOWS DIFFERENCE. HAPPY, UNHAPPY. LAUGH,
CRY. LIFE . . . LIFE, DEATH. EVERYTHING SOMETIMES
ONE, SOMETIMES ANOTHER. AND ANOTHER. YOU LEARN,
DOCTOR LEARN, BENJY LEARN, GOOD. DOCTOR PLAYS WITH
YOU, JAY, BENJY, NOT GOOD, NOT HAPPY. YOU LEARN
BENJY. JAY LEARN BENJY. BENJY NOT CARE ABOUT DOC-
TOR. WE LEARN EVERYTHING WE NEED, GO BE HAPPY
WHERE WE WERE, ON RINGS AND PLANETS AND STARS AND
THINGS. FORGET DOCTOR THEN. BE HAPPY.

Happy? Be happy? If you want to see the stars,
that makes three of us . . . happy! Christ almighty
and Shiva's flaming teeth, you've gotten me sounding like some country boy! Next thing we'll be
planting gardens and rooting out weeds and living
in mud huts and . . . and whatever they do out
there. How would we ever get to the stars if we'd
all done that all the time? I wonder . . . anyway,
Benjy, for whatever it's worth it's a deal.

GOOD IDEA.

We're going to get get along. You think like a spacer already!

I THINK BECAUSE I AM.

I'll drink to that!

CHAPTER SEVEN

"WHY ALERT ME by these warnings, these puerile warnings, Mr Parker?" Dr Brian said.

Parker's face in the visiphone did not change expression. "You're using those people, doctor, and I know it, and you know it. Now you know I know. Somehow that seems fair to me, if incomprehensible."

"Bah. You talk like a Naturalist. I've no time for such by-waters."

"Yet you continue to allow me this conversation. Could this be because you feel a fundamental uneasiness about your actions?"

"No, sir, my uneasiness is centered entirely around yours, whether you believe it or not. Your meddling into my private affairs has become offensive; frankly, I am taping this and my sole hope is that you slip and say something about which I may take more direct action."

"I wouldn't," Parker said, and his smile was slow and not very heartening.

"May I ask why?"

"Your subjects have been in your tender care over six months. Standard recuperation time, maximum, has been three months."

"Twice the problem, Mr Parker. Scarcely a circumstance to excite any interest in or out of the medical profession."

"Your subjects have reached a degree of integration—"

"Mr Parker," Dr Brian said, reaching a decision on some inaccessibly subconscious level. "One: Benjamin Tyler's body is in my direct legal care, and medical supervision over him is entirely my responsibility. Two: Miss Rost's cousins refuse to acknowledge that my patient is Jailyn Rost. They may or may not be on proper legal ground, but that has not yet been decided, and as yet the preponderance of court precedents is on my side in this. As for three, consider the finances of Joe Winslow. Everything he had saved has gone, sunk into costs. I did not like to require the money, but medicine has always been a poor relation to the more dramatic sciences, and it seems somehow appropriate to me that *some* money made in space is coming back to benefit life and knowledge here on Earth. At any rate, Mr Winslow is now technically a pauper, which again puts him under my direct jurisdiction as his medical supervisor."

"You aren't really interested in discussing the matter, are you, doctor?"

"Not really, sir, no. There are a number of vital new experiments that must be tried out as soon as possible. Why do you persist?"

"My employer is most interested in such reports of the progress of your experiments as I have obtained."

"Ah, yes, Templeton Kinsolving. No wonder your articles on Miss Rost have never appeared."

Parker's smile was still hardly reassuring. "He is rather intensely interested in the practical questions surrounding the problem of immortality, and thinks your researches may produce new leads. I am dubious, but I do my job, and I learn things. If I learn much more . . ."

Dr Brian felt anger—but quelled it immediately. Kinsolving! Now *there* was something he hadn't thought of. . . . "I cannot spare any further time at this period of my patients' development," he stated firmly. He reached for the cutoff plate.

Parker had time for a mock salute; then his sardonic features disappeared from Dr Brian's screen.

"Immortality," he thought a moment. "Preposterous. But this Parker has at last given me the means to rid myself of him. . . ."

For a moment he wondered at the flavor of that last thought, pondering its implications. "Science. Knowledge." The words sounded solid, secure, reasonable, important, as he said them aloud.

He turned back to his visiphone and began the difficult process of contacting a multimillionaire.

BENJY SAY DON'T EAT ASPARAGUS. BENJY THROW UP.

Winslow put down the forkful of asparagus in his left hand and sighed, while Jailyn reached for and picked up a glass of milk.

I told you he'd never go for it, Jailyn thought.

Sure, Winslow thought, but it didn't hurt to try. I thought maybe when he got a taste of how much I *love* asparagus—

BENJY SAY NO. BENJY HATE ASPARAGUS.

Frankly, I don't like it that much myself.

And then there's that little block Benjy's got against rare meat. You don't like that any better than I do. Well-done meat . . . feh. Aren't we all supposed to be cooperating all over the place these days?

BENJY COOPERATE.

Sure. Now, about that rare steak we tried to order last night?

BENJY THROW UP RAW MEAT. DON'T LIKE RARE MEAT.

BENJY NOT LIKE STRANGE FOODS JAY LIKE, JOE LIKE, BUT EAT MOST OF IT. NOT ASPARAGUS, NOT RAW MEAT.

And there you have it, ladies and gentlemen—fair's fair, Joe, bite the bullet.

But not the asparagus. Ok, ok, I won't go on about it any longer. It's just that . . . well, you know.

It's getting dull here, yes. Do you think we should try bracing the good doctor some more about letting us the hell out?

Dunno. I'd be easier in my mind about it if he'd ever let us have visitors. Problems . . . maybe no one wants to see us because they aren't interested; maybe they don't because we've caused a nation-wide revulsion against transplants; or maybe *he* wont let anyone in to hear our possible complaints. So if we want to leave . . . maybe its dangerous out there, or maybe he simply won't want to let us out. Will that do for openers?

Cold feet already, huh?

BENJY FEET NOT COLD.

Way of speaking, Benjy. I mean I'm wondering about our safety.

BENJY NEVER SAFE OUTSIDE. ALWAYS HURT HERE, HURT THERE, THEN CRY, AND MOMMY BRING ME BACK. THEY BRING ME BACK TO EXERCISE PLACE TOO, LATER. THAT WAS WHERE I FELL. BENJY REMEMBER. THEY SEND YOU DOWN TO OLD THINGS IN YOUR MIND, BENJY GO ALONG INTO OLD THINGS IN HIS MIND. BENJY REMEMBER.

Bunch of mystic stuff again. I don't—hey! some-one's coming in, someone new!"

". . . I suppose perhaps the best patient—or patients—I've ever had, Mr Kinsolving, as far as cooperation is concerned. Do everything I ask them to, hardly a murmur or a question. And with the equipment you could provide . . ."

Dr Brian was speaking animatedly to a tall thin elderly man whose conservatively cut, dark red suit was covered from neck to hands to special hospital shoes with transparent protective film.

Nurse Kim came to the bed-hospital and smiled down. "I see you're both up. Interested in meeting one of the richest men in the country?"

Hah! I met him once—pleasant sort on the surface, hateful the moment you get underneath. Determined.

"Uh," Joe said, trying to respond through Jailyn's thoughts, "what's the talk about equipment?"

"The nice man may buy Dr Brian some advanced devices for studying transplant results—specifically for your case, since you started being awake at the same times."

If she doesn't knock off that cutesy talk, I'll—

Come on, might as well give a try at being nice. If Kinsolving buys Brian a lot of special equipment, maybe that'll make Brian a little happier.

Or a little more determined to hold on to us. . . .

Tomorrow we can ask nasty leading questions; today, I have this thought that we should bend with the breezes, ok?

"You're showing off our new shtick, eh?" Jailyn said. "It takes a bit out of us to try to carry on a conversation when we're both up." But she manipulated controls, and the bed-hospital gently deposited the Tylerbody in an upright position. Tylerbody took a slightly shaky step forward.

"Ah, sir," said Dr Brian with excessive eagerness, "we *are* in luck! They're usually deeply engrossed in their studies at this time of day and, well, one thing they seem to resent is having their studies broken in upon. Hm, can't say I really blame them, hate it myself, but duty calls, and all that."

My God, he's blathering on today!

Kinsolving means money which means more research which means far far happier Dr Brian; of course he's

*blathering! He's so nervous it's a marvel he can stand
up as well as we can!*

"Yes," said Kinsolving. His white hair belied the
smooth skin on his long narrow face. Black eyes peered
sharply at the Tylerbody.

Then Kinsolving slowly extended a hand. "Bit irregular, this situation, eh? Templeton Kinsolving's my
name." The accompanying smile was quite perfunctory.
"How may I most conveniently address you without
being . . . well, without being discourteous?"

"I'm Jailyn Rost," Tylervoice said huskily, and

"I'm Joe Winslow," Tylervoice said sturdily, and
Tylerbody hand went out to meet Kinsolving's. Winslow continued. "I'm afraid neither of us can tell you
anything startlingly new, at least at the time. But we're
adjusting to it, as you can no doubt tell."

"Remarkable," said Kinsolving, "truly remarkable. I
did not really believe that such a situation could be
functionally resolved; this is really most heartening. If,
Dr Brian, you can offer a program of further progress
along these lines, I would frankly now consider that
as quite satisfactory justification for my investing, oh,
perhaps a very large amount of additional funding. For
that matter, I might take a personal interest; yes, that
might not be unjustified."

*You know, it's rather pitiful, seeing our good doctor
react with such obvious relief.*

I wonder. Could there be . . . Winslow's surge
of suspicion was cut short. Kinsolving was sticking his
hand out again.

"Let me repeat that I am impressed, quite impressed.
But I do not wish to tire you, or keep you from your
studies."

"Conversation when we're both up still is rather
draining for us," Jailyn said, truthfully enough.

Kinsolving nodded, and this time he actually appeared sympathetic. "Quite, quite. Well, I won't tax

you any further, today; but I imagine I may be around to visit again. Dr Brian gave me strict orders this visit was to remain brief, and I perceive I am already being cued. Thank you so much, Miss Rost, Mr Winslow. Er, Benjy, too, if he . . . if you can hear me, Benjy."

BENJY HEAR. WHO IS STRANGE MAN?

Hush, dear, he can't hear you. He's a . . . a nice man who wants to . . . to help us. I think.

BENJY UNDERSTAND. I THINK. NICE MAN SHOULD BE HAPPY.

Jailyn laughed, a rather grotesque effect with the Tylervoice. "Benjy thinks Mr Kinsolving is a nice man and wishes him happiness."

"Wishes me *happiness?*" Kinsolving almost smiled. "Country talk. But no matter. The question now is— well, but there are no more questions to ask you for now, I suppose. Thank you again for the privilege of meeting you. Good day."

Templeton Kinsolving III turned on his heels and strode out of the room, followed by Dr Brian.

You talk to nursie, ok? I think a little probing? But it only makes me lecherous when we're alone together; confusion factor.

Oh, sure, alone together—just the four of us. Charming picture! You, me, Benjy, and the sex idol of the Tenth Lower Level of New Bellevue.

Winslow, feeling Tylerbody's weariness, sighed and eased back into the bed-hospital, which slowly reclined to 10° off the horizontal.

"Well, now," Jailyn said to Miss Kim conversationally; the nurse looked up from the console, an indefinable look on her face. "Who the devil *is* Templeton Kinsolving III? And what is his interest in us?"

Miss Kim looked faintly disapproving. "Miss Rost, you were a rich woman—*are* a rich woman, I suppose. I find it hard to believe you don't know the man who established the first successful mining operations in the Mindinao Deep forty years ago."

"Oh, I know about how he made his money, well enough. I suppose I know more than a little about anyone who's worth over, say, ten million solits. But even at that price, Miss Kim, there are rather a number of people; so I can't say I understand him enough to know why he's interested in a dual brain transplant."

Miss Kim walked to the bed and looked down at the Tylerbody with that indefinable look on her face. "Kinsolving, unhappily for him, is one of those unfortunate men for whom age-rate reduction does not work. He's sixty and has been hoping for ten years for some modification to be discovered, but time's running out and he knows it. He can't stand the idea that his own contemporaries are going to be pushing a hundred when he's liable to have been in his grave for twenty years. Naturally he's interested in transplants."

"He's not bloody likely to get a chance at one, now, is he?" Winslow said, "First off, they don't take when they're that old. I know that much. And the few transplants that *are* made aren't just for old geezers wanting to squeeze out a few more years of their existence—rich or not."

Miss Kim shook her head. "If Kinsolving sinks twenty or thirty million solits into Dr Brian's current studies, do you think it so unlikely that something might be worked out? At any rate, I'm glad you handled him so well."

She's got that funny look in her eyes again, the way she always does these days when she looks at you.

Us.

You. Anyway, I'm going to . . .

"How closely can you follow what Joe and I are thinking about, these days?"

Miss Kim avoided blushing. "You mean sex? I can tell it's been on Joe's mind quite a bit lately, if that's what you're getting at. Certain lines of thought are always more noticeable, especially when one is . . . familiar with the subject in question."

"What are you talking about?" Winslow demanded, uneasily. "I thought we were talking about Kinsolving. We weren't going to go into that . . . that other subject for a long time."

"Never mind," Jailyn said immediately. "Feminine curiosity at work."

Miss Kim smiled. "So now you know."

"Yes, dear," said Jailyn. "Now I understand."

"Well, I sure as hell don't," Winslow said truculently, "but right now I'm more interested in what this Kinsolving's up to. I mean, if he puts money into Brian's hand, there's no telling how much longer he's going to want to keep us on tap . . . what did you say, ten years?"

"I didn't mean you, I meant him. But of course it'll be a long time yet you'll be in here being studied; you knew that already."

Miss Kim smiled to take the sting out of her words; suddenly Joe realized without knowing how that she *was* smiling at him, not at Jailyn. "Uh-oh," he said, "that's where it's at, eh? You've twigged I'm getting, uh, a, uh, hangup on, uh . . ."

"On my fair body? Don't worry about it," Miss Kim said, her smile warmer. "Nurses get used to it; some become quite disappointed if it doesn't happen."

"But, I mean, well, the circumstances, I mean, special—"

"Benjy Tyler is a strong handsome young lad, with plenty of good healthy virile instincts," said Miss Kim. "Don't apologize."

BENJY LIKE NICE WOMAN!

Miss Kim held a readout plate; glancing at it, she smiled her secret smile again. "No matter what final resolutions come about," she said, "you *can* see why Dr Brian feels there is so much to learn, can't you?"

She's teasing, Joe thought accusingly.

Of course! Jailyn thought back, amusement rising in

her till she almost laughed out loud. *And I don't blame her! If I were in her shoes I'd be fascinated by the . . . by the chance to . . . well, never mind.*

But Jailyn giggled aloud, while Joe Winslow went back to private, walled-off, optimistic thoughts. . . .

CHAPTER EIGHT

Got to try something new, Jailyn, that's all there is to it. I'm so goddamned bored I've already figured out seven ways to kill the good doctor without anybody even knowing he's been murdered. Enough is enough.

Well, I suppose you had something in mind.

Consider this: Miss Kim can tell whenever I'm interested in matters pertaining to sex, as you might say, and—

It's nice you finally noticed.

Do I detect a chilly tone?

She has a letch for this body; I spotted it before she said anything the other day.

So did I; how many secrets do you think you can keep, inside one skull?

Hah. I've kept a few safe from you, anyway. And I notice you never think too much about the women in your past life, either.

Let's not go into that, what say? It could be summed up that I've not been entirely fortunate in my love life—and I'd hazard a guess the same's true for you, for all your money.

Men think money's such an answer for things—it is, too, but not for men and women. In their relationships. And I don't think we need to go into this again for a while, do you? It's a little difficult . . . back to Nursie and her sexual ambivalences . . .

I'll tell you one way we might make some progress in getting out of here, finding out what their plans for us may really be, all that. But you won't much care for it, I'm sure, and—

Make love to her?

You are a woman of countless surprises and of great perspicacity; exactly. And what do you think of the idea?

Frankly, I loathe, hate, and fear the idea; but it looks like the only good chance we can opt for.

Uh, you could maybe wall yourself off while it's, er, going on—you know. I know *I* can concentrate on other matters if we're both up and you're talking with someone, at least if I really put my mind to it. And I know you can do the same thing, pretty much, because I've tried testing your resistance then, and I've bounced.

I certainly intend to try to wall myself off, yes. I may have picked a resonance in your mind, matching one of my problems reasonably well—on one level, you've got a masculinity worry, though on other levels you're correctly aware that there is no reason for it. Tylerbody took an unexpected deep breath at Jailyn's instinctive command. *Well, I have something like it, a femininity . . . doubt, if that's the right verbalization. Comes of mucking about in spaceships and trying to outthink supercomputers, and having an . . . well, an erratic love life, if you must know.*

There was a pause in the interchange; Joe did not push her.

The idea of caressing another woman's body, she continued slowly, *makes me uneasy—partly because there is that level on which the idea is fascinating, utterly fascinating. Even lascivious, if you'll pardon my blushes. Oh, well, all humans have a touch of this problem; most of them don't like to admit it, that's all. It* only tends to get a little exaggerated, out of hand, aberrative if you will, in fields like space travel—you and I both. At any rate the idea of caressing is difficult enough to contemplate; and as for . . . for . . .

Her trailing-off thought was swamped in a complete image that sprang up in her mind and was immediately picked up by Joe—a naked man and woman just on the verge of the central act of lovemaking. The image was complete with the tactile messages of the flesh, the eager anticipation, the odors, sights, sounds, and overtones of the act—and woven in with the visionary glimpse was the flavor of Jailyn's innate shock, recognizing herself potentially the *man* in this scene. . . .

Tylerbody whistled, for Joe.

You've made your point, I guess. So I can expect you to go off and count sheep. I don't know, you might even say I feel a little . . . relieved. Rich imagery of the actual Jailyn, swathed in dream-green cloth, looking over Joe's shoulder as he made love to Miss Kim. . . .

BENJY SAYS HOW DID YOU DO THAT?

Huh? *Do what?* Simultaneous babble of puzzlement. BENJY MAKE PRETTY SOUND NOW. BENJY NEVER MADE PRETTY SOUND BEFORE. HOW?

What pretty sound, Benjy? Winslow did not have to make an effort to avoid feeling irritated; by now he was used to Benjy's occasionally incredibly irrelevant interruptions.

The Tylerbody lips pursed suddenly, alarming both Joe and Jailyn; THAT SOUND, came Benjythoughts. BUT BENJY STILL CAN'T DO IT. HOW?

Whistling! Joe, he—

Like this, Benjy. See, you just go . . .

And Joe Winslow slowly pursed Tylerlips, placed tongue just so, expelled air, and thereby emitted a rather unsatisfactory whistle.

See? Follow that? He threw an aside at Jailyn with a mental grin. Damn, Jailyn, teaching myself to whistle at twenty-seven. I want to tell you, it's *weird*, lady!

BENJY UNDERSTAND NOW. LIPS AND BREATHPUSH OUT. NOBODY TOLD ME BEFORE. COULDN'T ASK. . . .

From Benjy came what for him was a thought-sigh; then the Tylerbody pursed its lips again suddenly and a whoosh of air came out, nothing like a whistle.

Tongue too, Benjy, like so. . . . And Joe went through the motions again, thinking out instructions as he went; then he whistled once more.

Then the Tylerbody whistled quaveringly—by itself, as it seemed to Joe and Jailyn; and again a kind of alarm unnerved them momentarily.

Uh . . . Benjy, uh, that's it. That's good. We'll teach you more in a little while. But . . . you mustn't do that when . . . when people are around, unless you ask us first.

BENJY NO-NO WHISTLE? Undertones of sadness were dampened unexpectedly quickly by automatic energizers in the bed-hospital.

Joe, let me try to explain to him—Benjy, when we have company you shouldn't . . . shouldn't "take over" like that. It . . . it might make one of us . . . look funny.

Hold on, someone *is* coming in.

BENJY QUIET. BENJY HAPPY NOW. BENJY CAN WHISTLE. BENJY WHISTLE WHEN YOU LET HIM. BENJY UNDERSTAND. BENJY LOVE MOMMYDADDY.

Joe whistled

—and Miss Kim came in the door simultaneously with the whistle. "Signs of true life and intelligence at last, eh?" she said, with a little laugh. "I wondered when you were really going to notice."

"Believe me," Joe said fervently, "I noticed, a long time ago. But I've got this next-door neighbor, you know? Doesn't make things any easier for me. I think . . . I think maybe she's jealous or—"

Jealous! Why, you—

Shut up or you'll blow it the moment she checks
the readout. Quit; go away; let me deal with her;
you ever seduce a woman before? Then lay off!

Christ, no, I never—She broke off; but there was a
subliminal chuckle. *I know how it's done, just the same!
But get on with it; I'll go away somewhere and contemplate the navel I used to have. . . .*

"—or something," Joe continued; the pause for
thought interchange had been almost unnoticeably
short.

Miss Kim started to walk to the monitor console.

"Hey," Joe said, sitting up on the edge of the bed,
"no fair reading my mind while I'm complimenting
you! 's cheating!"

In spite of herself, the chief nurse blushed, and
turned away from the console before seeing the readout. She started to make a gesture with her hand, but
it turned into a confused gesture trailing off into a
meaningless patting of her hair.

*I'd judge she hadn't really expected me to get on
with it, but thinks that now I might just be,* Joe shot
at Jailyn, forgetting his own stricture.

Your problem, Jailyn sent back from what felt like
the other end of a tunnel, a lengthening tunnel.

"Anyway," Joe continued, "I got my lady friend in
a snit at me, I guess. She's walled herself away studying
the navel she used to have, or something. So now I
can, er, talk to you, you know."

Joe breathed deeply; he was finding it not so easy to
get into the right mood.

Miss Kim ceased patting her hair and touched the
pocket over her left breast. Frowning slightly, she
pulled out a small notebook, glanced at it puzzledly as
if wondering how it had gotten there, and set it down
beside the console.

Then she looked straight at Joe's eyes. "I'm not
looking at the readout," she said, "I'm looking at you.
And I can still tell what you're thinking."

Joe grinned Tylerbody mouth and face, and felt, inside, that he must look pretty good, grinning, for Miss Kim immediately smiled—an oddly hesitant one, but a smile nonetheless.

"What am I thinking?" Joe said.

"You're lonely," she said immediately.

Joe blinked.

She was right.

And he hadn't realized it.

"Hey, that's my line," he said, shamelessly picking up the unplanned cue. "I'm not knocking Jailyn, you understand, but . . . well, it's not really the same thing." Which, he realized, was true! "Especially since we still have, well, problems getting along, communicating, *you* know."

"Of course I know," Miss Kim said, almost calmly. "It's my business to. But it all brings up a question . . ."

Joe eased himself off the edge of the bed.

He was dressed in the customary bright-orange boxing trunks—which he hated, and which were orange for visibility. Berserk patients still did occasionally attempt to run away; and inside or outside the hospital itself, the bright trunks were pure visibility.

"We're fencing," Joe said abruptly.

"Of course!" Miss Kim said, smiling again.

Then she walked toward the door.

"*Wait!*" Joe said, deeply alarmed. "Don't go yet, I want . . ."

His voice trailed off and he felt his face turn red.

She had locked the "medical privacy" mechanism on the only door to the room. Not even Dr Brian—short of an all-hospital emergency—would ordinarily attempt to enter. It was necessary for whole classes of tests and operations; patients could not operate the lock, however, no matter how much they craved privacy, since the lock was coded only to staff fingerprints.

Miss Kim turned back to Joe, and walked slowly toward him.

"Dueling is fun," she said, "when circumstances favor it. Right now, other circumstances would seem to apply. And your Miss Rost's being off somewhere is most definitely 'other circumstances,' since I'm well aware that most of the time she won't permit you to say anything to me you might really have wanted to say. But— now you can say it! Am I right?"

"Talking is fun too," Joe said.

Miss Kim frowned again.

Joe stepped forward, almost touching her. "When circumstances favor talking, that is . . . !"

And he put his arms around her and kissed her.

She tensed a moment in his arms; in spite of herself, as it seemed to Joe.

Then she moved, in his arms, closer to him, her lips eager against his.

For a moment Joe savored the femininity of her, pressed against him, the womansmell of her hair, the softness of her flesh; and under the uniform, nothing but her.

That was why she'd taken the small notebook out of her breast pocket, part of him realized with amusement and appreciation.

. . . and then it was as a gate rusted shut had burst open, and he and she were kissing each other frantically now, and he ran his right hand down the pressurezip that curved from the back of her neck around her left arm and down to the front hem of her short uniform skirt, and she shrugged her shoulders and the dress fell away from her completely, pooling whitely on the floor below her lovely ivory skin.

Time! Would they have time? he wondered frantically for a moment; then "Ah!" he gasped involuntarily with the sudden loveliness of her nakedness; then she was smiling and tugging at the boxing trunks until they lay on the floor beside the uniform.

"The restcouch," she said then. "Not the bed-hospital, I couldn't stand that."

"'S quite comfortable," Joe said equitably, knowing he shouldn't bother making the point, "but I understand what you mean."

"Shhhh!" she said with a little smile, touching a finger to his lips. "Life isn't all talking and thinking! It's feeling, too!"

"You're telling me it—"

He smiled and broke off, then reached for her once more as they stood beside the restcouch, wide and inviting.

Naked they held each other for a moment, then broke away and clambered eagerly onto the restcouch, and touched each other and kissed each other, moaning incoherently as they built their mutual needs as quickly as possible; and quickly then, because neither he nor she could stand more delay, he moved between her legs and they joined together in a joyful lovemaking. . . .

It was a bit more of a job than she'd bargained for, switching her attention away from the Tylerbody eyes when the nurse came into the room. Adrenalin was already coursing through Tylerbody with Joe's anticipation of the next minutes.

Without eyes sending her messages she would accept, she found her hearing sharpened—and that was no good, not with so many lascivious overtones only too obvious to Jailyn.

So she shut off hearing too.

Blind, deaf, she felt her—Tylerbody's, dammit—male arousal. New panic touched her.

And stayed.

Always before she had been able to disregard that, when it occurred. For a brief moment the possible realization that it might simply be her unwillingness to finally accept her present position flashed through her mind, but convoluted like the sentence necessary to convey the twisty flash of intuition.

Then the intuition had disappeared, leaving her back with a slowly growing panic. Usually she had her mind elsewhere while Joe handled ordinary male elimination functions, as she stiltedly phrased it to herself. Therefore she should be reasonably used to not-concentrating on the . . . the maleness of . . . of her body. . . .

Arousal had always been difficult for her to bear, though, even when it was routine, nonspecific; it wasn't that it simply reminded her of her irrevocable situation, she told herself, forgetting to remember the earlier insight. It was that it reminded her, every time, of the inevitable ordeal—Tylerbody making love to a woman.

Yet *why should that bother me so*, she thought distractedly, and her mind shifted away before she could focus on any more answers.

Stimulation . . . with an effort she drew her attention away now from sense of body—blind; deaf; bodiless.

Smell of girlhair—intolerable, accentuated.

She blanked that out, but at the same time she was now aware dimly that the two bodies in the room were now embracing for the first time.

Awareness, total . . .

. . . another touch of panic at that, but all was back under control. She *couldn't* give up all her awareness of what was happening, she *couldn't!* For, if she did, she knew suddenly, she would become unconscious— and then she would dream!

It took no effort to realize that she would of course simply dream about the one thing that was actually happening, to . . . yes, to her body: what it was doing right now.

And so there was, after all, no real escape from where she was. . . .

Taste—she hadn't blocked taste!

It was hopeless. Confused, erotic, painful, joyful,

and Miss Kim's own tongue now in her mouth, no no
no no *his* mouth she screamed to herself *his* mouth
not mine not mine no no no no but the tongue was
warm and moist and Tylerbody was breathing deeply
and moving arms and

—She shut out taste now, and touch again, and sight,
and hearing, and as much body sensation as she could
without falling unconscious into dreams of the present,
and tried to work out how some day she would find a
genius who would make her Earth room on Mars into
the epitome of all that man had meant so far, and

Miss Kim beside her on the bed, touching Jailyn's
body, grasping her maleness for a moment, then urg-
ing her into her with moans and gasps of anticipatory
pleasure, and the blood thundered gloriously in Jailyn's
brain and the taste of Miss Kim's tongue again, and
the touch of Miss Kim's beautiful smooth breasts in
her hands, and then inside inside inside and out in out
unbearable the pleasure the horror no no no she knew
not horror joy now but ohmygod whatdoesitmean what-
isthisifeeldontunderstand it'snotlikethisforawoman god-
godgod, o god, o god, o god, this building battering
warmsofthardglidingsmooth plunging joyness this girl-
thin lovelysweating beneathher o god

CHAPTER NINE

"WHAT MAKES YOU THINK I'll give you anything else besides my fair body," Miss Kim said smiling, as she sat beside Joe.

Her uniform was on, and he had his orange trunks back, and the door no longer on "medical privacy."

And Joe felt more than a little disappointed.

He had rather expected to be like a young stallion with this charming female beside him. His body was young and strong; he himself had been skilled in the restraints and recuperations of the body; but past a certain point the Tylerbody had more or less acted on its own. Not exactly Benjy; the body itself.

So it had lasted only a few minutes, and none of Joe's skilled restraint had been of any use, and the Tylerbody seemed disinclined to arouse itself again. He began to feel basically rather depressed about the whole thing, despite pleasant physical and mental aftereffects.

No, it hadn't been the way he'd expected—more like when he had been a schoolboy, making it for the first time with a wise young girl teacher, helpless (as he had felt those twelve years ago) in her hands, not to mention her body.

"I'm not demanding that much, you know," Joe answered. "I'll take anything I can get at this point, of course—information at least, up through complete aiding-and-abetting in our, hm, escape. Or if not, well, I've no regrets." (This last was not true; he wanted to spend hours in bed with this woman.) "But at the least, I'm curious, and rightfully so, I believe."

"Dr Brian has . . . determined ideas," said Miss Kim, snuggling a little closer to the handsome body beside her, and wondering about the principles of nursing off in one corner of her mind while the rest of her was still soaking in pleasant memories. "You've guessed already that he never had any intentions of letting anyone you know get in to see you. He had good sound reasons, true—but some were less so, which is not your business. Except, of course," she reflected, "that it is *all* your business, in a sense. Sanctity of the individual, and all. Honored in the breach in this case, I'm afraid."

Joe sighed and drew away from her slightly.

"But I'll tell you this," she went on. "There's a feisty little man who's been getting quite upset over Dr Brian's lack of interest in letting him in to see . . . Miss Rost. That's breaking a confidence or something, I suppose, but I can't see any harm in just letting you know you *do* have a friend out there. Dr Brian wants you to remain here not only physically, unfortunately for you, but polarized here mentally too, as it were. *He* regards you as his private experiment, of course."

"Something did give me that impression, yes; well, it's nice to know someone's interested out there, I suppose. Makes it—"

"—worth the effort?" she said, and grinned at him, rubbing her hands over his hard young chest and observing the ripple of his muscles, Tylerbody muscles.

"Effort!" Joe chuckled, reminiscing. He kissed her, then stood up and stretched.

There was a knock at the door—unusual, since Dr Brian and Miss Kim never bothered.

The nurse got up and opened the door.

It was Les Parker, though Joe did not recognize him. Parker was holding a suitcase.

"Not much time to talk," Parker said immediately, putting the suitcase down. "Saw Brian down the next hall—he's sure to be here in a minute. I'm getting you out of here—if you want to get out, that is." He did not heavily emphasize the sarcasm in his voice.

Tylerbody grinned, and Joe felt Jailyn present, watching now. *Had she been, earlier?* he wondered, to himself.

Jailyn, this the one you knew   he shot at her. You want to take over talking to him? Did you catch what Miss Kim was saying?

Yes on all three, she answered, biting the thought off while only too aware that her roiled emotions were already spilling over the quasi walls between their minds. She tried to force them back once more, succeeding only in intensifying them. *Oh, shit,* she thought then, harshly cutting through the emotion. *I . . . saw . . . the whole thing. I'm upset. I felt the whole thing —upset isn't the word. But that I don't want to talk about for now, ok?*

Agreed, Joe answered immediately, eager to help her calm down—the sensation of her conflicting emotions warring along through his own mind was distinctly unpleasant.

"Hi, Les," Jailyn said in husky Tylerbody voice. "We'll take whatever help we can, and tell you everything we can that's decent into the bargain. The only questions are, how do we get out of here, and when?"

Parker kneeled and opened the suitcase rapidly, displaying a complete set of crisp new clothes. The wrinkles in its paper disappeared as Parker lifted the suit out. "Get this on—quickly. When Brian gets here— and I'll bet that's pretty soon—we'll deal with him."

Miss Kim stepped back several paces and raised the back of her hand to her mouth. "Deal with him?" she whispered. "What . . . what do you mean?"

Parker frowned impatiently as the Tylerbody clumsily attempted to don the new suit. "It's psychologically important you be dressed to leave *before* he arrives. I give it another minute uppermost. Come on!"

You *do it, then*, Jailyn thought, despairing of integrating smoothly with Benjy's clumsy habits. *I just realized one thing I never learned. Seems they make men's clothes more different than women's all the time.*

I'm a little rusty myself, Joe responded, finally getting the shoes, legs, and arms of the suit all on him. Parker stepped forward and zipped up the invisible pressureseams while Joe struggled to get the colorful neckband right.

He gave up as Parker finished with the seams, and let the older man adjust the neckband fit, and the door opened then, and Dr Jon Brian stood there, his face red with unaccustomed anger.

"So you finally got inside the wards, eh, you sneaking little—" Dr Brian stopped and took in the freshly suited Tylerbody. Joe smiled as if he hadn't a care in the world. "Now then," Brian said in a dangerous voice, "what's this?"

"Your former patient, or patients," said Parker. "Now, then. I am quite aware that they are medically totally recovered. They are in fact fit not only to leave the intensive-care area, but the whole damned hospital. Damn your arrogance, sir!" Parker went on spiritedly, "and damn the arrogance of this whole bureaucracy! That you actually think you have the moral right to imprison these people the way you have, in this age of . . . of supposed justice we have supposedly achieved . . . well, never mind all that. Bureaucracy works both ways—and so does hanky-panky.

"You might as well step out of that doorway, doctor," Parker finished, with as imperative a gesture as he could manage, considering his slight figure.

"Why?" said Dr Brian, his voice calm and his face once more impassive.

A reasonable question under the circumstances, wouldn't you say? Joe thought wryly, but Jailyn did not answer; he felt the stress in her mind, wondered if he could do anything, then returned attention to the two men.

Parker reached inside his bolero, and Miss Kim shrank back several more steps, every tensed muscle in her body clearly anticipating a gun.

Parker's hand brought out a sheaf of papers. "Here you are, doctor—your copies of the various orders I have gone to some trouble to obtain. More than some, considering that my employer cut my funds after his first visit here a month ago. You will find them all quite in order, and quickly verifiable. There is, in short, no longer any least justification for your further obstruction of our progress out of this monument to misery, sir, and it would indicate a singular gentility on your part if you would now simply step aside and permit us to go our inevitable way."

Dr Brian stared at the papers that had been thrust into his unwilling hands. He looked at the top one, blinked, looked at the next one, blinked again. Then he shuffled quickly through the rest of them; there were half a dozen complete sets.

He walked silently to the computer console and placed the whole stack of papers on the in-tray. He punched instructions to New York Prime Computer, Verifications Bloc—scan the documents, verify them, summarize them. Then he looked up at the screen.

The only reason the answer wasn't already there before his eyes could reach the screen was that it took the mechanical sorters inside the console finite seconds to shuffle through all the papers with deft artificial "fingers." But after that the scanned information went down to Prime, deep under Manhattan's surface, surrounded and protected by a great deal of granite—and nanoseconds thereafter the answer was glowing on Dr Brian's readout.

"Authenticated documents requiring release of patients known colloquially as Joe Winslow, Jailyn Rost, and Benjy Tyler, identification numbers . . ." and a great spew of figures tumbled across the screen which no one bothered to look at; nobody ever bothered to look at them. That job was safe to leave to the computers; it didn't need any double-checking by humans, who tended to get confused after the first dozen digits anyhow.

Dr Brian sat slowly down in the console seat and rubbed a hand over his brow. Miss Kim took several hesitant steps toward him, then stopped in confusion, looking about at the two other male figures in the room.

Then her face pinched with anger. "All right then," she flared, "they're genuine. But we can still hold you up with outprocessing, long enough so that I'll willingly bet you half my year's income against yours those orders will be officially countermanded within twenty hours, and—"

Parker broke her confused flow with a gesture, and brought out another sheet of paper, which he handed to Dr Brian. "Should Miss Kim's impulse find an echo in you, Dr Brian, I suggest you read over that copy of a summary of certain other information I . . . came across, shall we say?"

Dr Brian took the sheet, glaring at Parker before he turned his attention to it; then his hand shook slightly.

Nonetheless he skimmed over the whole sheet before looking back at Parker. "Yes," he said then, and his voice was steady if his hands were not. "I suppose that your possession of this summary of my connection with Boardman ten years ago means you are also in possession of the proofs to back it up?"

"The summary is true, is it not? How much verification do you think the deaders would need, if a strong enough hint reached them that one of Boardman's men was still alive and practicing—"

Dr Brian stood. "I will not stoop to threatening you in return."

"Doctor, you needn't bother," said Parker. "I've already had an impressive batch of threats from my employer, my former employer. Fortunately, old Kinsolving never realized how far I'd progressed before he took his personal interest in the matter directly to you."

Dr Brian looked away, his eyes absently drifting to the readout, which was glowing softly, blankly.

He said nothing, even as they silently walked out; and Chief Nurse Kim stood blinking tears away.

CHAPTER TEN

"GOD DAMN your eyes, Al, but you've turned into a pompous son of a bitch. When did you ever know as much about the multiwave as I did? And you have the nerve to quote *security* regulations at me?"

Joe Winslow slammed two strong Tylerbody hands palms down on Al Zink's desk. Zink cocked his head uneasily as Tylerbody stood up.

"Now, look here, uh, Joe, *I* don't make the regulations, you know that. You hate to have someone give you that line, I know—Christ knows I hear it often enough myself. But it's no less true for being unpleasant."

Al Zink shrugged, and Tylerbody leaned forward, looming over Zink's slight frame.

He's lost a lot of weight—looks like even Parker could beat him up now!

How did you know—never mind. You're right. But let me alone a minute—I've got to push this guy a little .

The Supervisor of the Multiwave Transmission Experiments Department involuntarily shrank back a little from the threatening figure, so strange to him but which spoke so familiarly to him.

"There's no need for you to take it out on me, either," Zink added, seeing the anger on the young face. "Now, I've got a tape on our conversation, and I promise I'll have my girls make up all the necessary forms, applications, all that. But, Joe, you wanted it direct and I'm giving it to you direct. It won't go past the next level up from me, and I know it, and you know it. And we may both know it's pure horseshit, but look at the thing this way, too. Who are you?

"Yes, yes, yes, Joe, you have a good memory, I believe you. I believe you're . . . Joe Winslow's brain, Joe Winslow's excellent and highly skilled and very knowledgeable brain, still packed with a lot of valuable information and capabilities, and all that. You'd pass all the retests routinely—you wouldn't have shown up here if you weren't sure of that.

"And I *know* you're Joe Winslow because you remember things about the time we were on Martian dzingush and didn't even know it—things nobody else would know or would bother to learn; sure. That's fine, as far as it goes.

"But look at you!" Zink gestured at the irate figure before him, as if to an audience standing at his huge picture window overlooking downtown Manhattan.

"You don't *look* like Joe Winslow. You don't have Joe Winslow's fingerprints. Now stop glaring at me; I'm not trying to hoover you. I can even give you a little information, maybe—as I understand it you've been having problems ever since you got out of the hospital, and it's been over a month." Zink smiled. It was a thin, self-satisfied smile.

Joe Winslow remembered when Al Zink's smiles were broad and happy; supervisory work for six years had pinched him in away from life.

"I took an interest in your case, Joe," Zink said, now almost unctuous. "Just like everyone else when the headlines broke; but then people lost interest again, the way they do. But I decided to check out a few things. I've got security obligations, working on this level, and I was wondering about your Dr Brian. As far as security, he's clean—though I gather the deaders might be very unhappy with him. But that's up to them; I don't hoover *anyone*."

"Brian's irrelevant," Joe said, trying to keep irritation out of his voice, and not succeeding.

"I know that—now," Zink said, making no effort to hide his own irritation. "And then there's Templeton Kinsolving. Did you know about him?"

"We met him," Joe said. "That's about all."

"Your Mr Parker was a good workmanlike . . . arranger, fortunately for you, because if Kinsolving had heard about the release before it went through, you'd still be there."

"We were a little lucky there," Joe admitted grudgingly. "Parker was writing for one of Kinsolving's papers—that's how Kinsolving first got interested in us. Luckily Parker didn't check upstairs before trying to finagle us out. I'd really rather not think about it!"

"Well, now, I have a feeling Mr Kinsolving does not want to die, and that he feels that professional study of your . . . situation? . . . will somehow aid him in his feverish desire to extend his life. How? How should I know? I'm not a medical man, hate the whole messy business. Blood makes me vomit. *You* remember."

Zink flashed a look at Joe; an odd quirky smile lit his face for a moment.

Joe grinned back at him. "Yeah. Especially when it's blue with dzingush!"

Zink sighed, shaking his head ruefully. "Well," he continued, "Kinsolving's been talking to people, spreading around a little money—and he has a great deal. Have you tried to get any of your money yet?"

"My accounts were wiped out by the expenses of all the operations, since Transfed takes about six years to process claims. I'm told I may see some money by the sixties. Jailyn hasn't really made a serious attempt at getting at her accounts, though that'll be our next stop. Parker's been carrying us since we got out, but that's why we're here—we're tired of sponging."

"It boils down to the legal question of whether you really exist, Joe. And that too may take years—especially if Kinsolving has anything to say about it, which from all indications he certainly means to."

Tylereyes shut, then opened; Joe allowed himself to sigh and sit back down slowly.

"Let's hear the rest of it," Joe said after a few deep breaths.

"There's not that much," Zink said carefully. "Legally, you *may* still be Benjy Tyler. You may even be Joe Winslow and you may be Jailyn Rost—legally, legally. Now, that's a word Security's very hung up on; it's always been like that. *You* know. What more can I say? You've got your problems, I've got mine, and right now our problems are intertwined, it seems. What I'm trying to say is, that our mutual problems, we can't do anything about them, see?

"I'd like to have you back. You're a good man, one of the top two dozen or so in your branch of the field, and I still envy you. I can't cut it in the field, I know that; that's why I'm just as happy to be shuffling papers behind this desk. I level with you, you see? But."

"But. Security. Kinsolving. Threedee scare talk about the multimind menace. Ok, Al, ok. I won't leap across the desk and punch you in the face. I'll be civilized about it. I won't set fire to your office or rape your secretary or Get Revenge some other way." Joe sagged in his chair a little, then went on, his voice listless. "You're making an honest effort to get through to me, and . . . and I appreciate it, even if I have my reservations about—"

"About my courage, about not fighting for an old fellow dzingush zonker? All that stuff? Ok, you've got the right, Joe. You may even *be* right. Still, I know a

lot more about the art of the possible than you do—
you were always too pigheaded to listen to reason,
and . . ."

Zink paused, and looked out his window for a moment at the unfinished stub of the other World Trade
Tower. Neither building had gotten past the seventieth
floor when the plaguewars and Changes hit, and eco-
nomics had permanently kept them from completion
when things began later to swing back to something
like what they had been before.

"But what the hell," Zink finished, turning back to
Joe. "You're grown up, you don't need advice, right?"

Joe smiled ruefully. "I'm not so sure about that,
these days. But I need a job a lot more, and that's a
fact. Jailyn and I are getting stupefied with boredom,
just sitting around and—"

"Miss Rost, yes, there's that other legal problem.
Clearances are funny things, you know."

"Huh. Don't I. But Jailyn's right in with government
computer work—has more clearances than I do!"

"And so that's no problem, right? Well, it is." Smug-
ness returned to Al Zink's voice. "Need-to-know. She
doesn't have multiwave clearances, you don't have
computer clearances—at least, not on the levels we're
really talking about."

Tylerbody slumped again. "Do you know, for the first
time I really believe you. Of course it wouldn't make
any difference to Security that we're demonstrably not
traitors—just locked into the same head now. I believe they expect we'd spy on each other under such
circumstances. I wonder who they think we'd tell the
secrets to."

Al Zink nodded, a bit taken aback by Winslow's obvious and sudden acceptance. "To work on computers,
she doesn't need to know about your problems with
the z-r-v functions. And you don't need to know about
the latest ego-precipitation work with the Yaletron.

Security simply won't have that, and yes, of course, it's
silly-ass, and it's also the way it is, and you know it and
I know it.

"I don't like to say this, Joe, but you're sort of . . .
well, I'd say you've lost."

"Lost."

Tylerbody sat slumped, and blinked a few times, and
minds pondered wordlessly the words that had been
spoken, and then it was Tylerbody standing up and
sighing again. Joe said: "You're right. I *have* lost. Up
till now. Up *through* now, if you will. But one thing's
for sure—I'm not done yet, and if that sounds like a
rerun from an old Skycycle Gang script, well, I suppose
it probably is. But there's this difference: I'm not in a
Skycycle Gang script, though it feels that way sometimes. I'm not done, and I mean it."

Winslow felt Tylerbody about to sag suddenly, and
searched for energy reserves to hold up until they'd
left.

For a moment Al Zink's shiny new office disappeared
and there was only pure perception of the vast emptiness that was the solar system—and the multiwave
generators on their transplanted asteroids once more
glimmered in their orbit like a necklace of tiny, incredibly brilliant jewels.

Then it was over, and Al was talking. ". . . and you
know, I'm about as far up the ladder as I'm going,
Joe, I don't mind telling you. I'm five years older than
you are, and all my old dreams of running the whole
show, I packed them away a long time ago. I take them
out every now and then, out of my memory, and look
at them like they were funny pictures in some old
photo album, flat, unreal; and then I put them back.
I accept where I am. You understand, this doesn't make
me happy. But I can be content with it."

Al's face was troubled; he *was* trying to be sympathetic.

Joe reached over the desk, offering Tylerhand to Zink, who took it after a startled moment.

From somewhere behind Zink's desk, a discreet buzzing punctuated Joe's hesitant attempt to thank him. "So long, Al, and thanks for the song and dance; it was a little easier to take coming from someone I knew once. If you'd been some ironfaced Scuttyfuck I think I *would* have tried to beat your face in, just for the pure joyous hell of it." And Joe grinned wryly; Jailyn was angrily trying to cut in. "No," he said aloud to her, and Zink shook his head confusedly several times. "We won't be back. Sleep easy tonight, Al, we won't come back and haunt you."

"That's a relief," Zink said, with pleasant acidity.

A light now began flashing on his desk. Zink frowned, looking at it; then he looked up, Tylerbody still looming over him.

"Uh," Zink said uncertainly, "I don't want to hustle you out of here, but I've got a priority call from field unit headquarters. New alignment tests, you understand. If you'll excuse me . . ."

Joe immediately walked to the door. He pressed his hand on the plate and it slid open; but he turned, hand still on the plate keeping the door open. Zink was already punching out an acceptance code on his desk console.

Jailyn made Tylervoice taut with anger. "Do you dare to tell me," she said levelly, "that you won't open up *any* of my accounts, not even my personal ones, on my direct authorization?"

The bank's vice president coolly eyed Tylerbody and said, voice chill, "We don't know who you are, and, if I may speak with some frankness, we don't really care. The legal point is clear—it was tentatively established some years ago. You don't have proper certification of identity; we are not required to do anything at all. I don't need to tell you this, but as several heirs of Jailyn Rost have already been contacted and have expressed their deep interest in these matters, you can see there is hardly any use in—"

"*Heirs?*" Jailyn made Tylervoice very soft, very dangerous. "My will specifies Jimmy Tungo, not that he needs any of my money. Who are these heirs?"

"Ah, er, I am not precisely at liberty to go into confidential details on the Rost, um, estate," said the vice president, and he diddled around with a lightpen.

"Oh, yes, you are. You can tell me who it is that's trying to promote himself into my—"

The vice president shook his head from side to side, with great emphasis. "No, sir, I do not know who you are, nor am I greatly interested. You have not got certification of identity and I am, hm, given to understand that you might find acquiring such certification rather difficult. This information is sufficient for me to base a decision on, and my position is quite clear to me. I will tell you nothing further."

He sat back, reaching for the topmost of a stack of papers on his desk as he did so.

Jailyn stood; the vice president gave no sign.

She leaned Tylerbody over the front of his desk. "When your Mr Kinsolving checks in with you again," Tylervoice said softly, "you can relay him this message from Jailyn Rost—I would not help him stay alive another minute, and may he die soon of the plagues of chestrot and ratmad."

The vice president blinked, looked up, but said nothing, not even at the plaguewar words people didn't often use.

"And as for you," she continued, knowing she was far too angry and should shut up, "may all your sons and daughters flee to the country before they reach sixteen—" She felt subliminal reactions to that thrust; and so she turned it, watching him wince. "*If they haven't already!*"

It was one of the great insults, when it hit home, since it conveyed full understanding of another's failings as a parent—which is to say as a human being, the customary failing of parents. This one, this vice president, knew he had failed, knew he would never understand why. Perhaps someone once had even told him what *that* meant; for it was the proof of his failure.

Which, Jailyn knew bitterly, was the sort of thing that produced a man like this—who could be bought by someone like Kinsolving.

She almost reached out for Joe then, because Kinsolving was beginning to frighten her, on a level she'd never been frightened at before. The man *did not want to die*, and since this was an age where there was, at last, some scientific promise that he needn't, it frightened her to realize that, to him, she represented *only* a chance for him to live—perhaps not even that, for there was no real proof anything could be learned from her experience to help Kinsolving. And nothing she thought or was concerned about meant a thing to him.

She wouldn't go to Joe; she couldn't take that constant flood of male thought overtones, that constant polarizing sexual notice that drove her frantically against the diminishing reefs of her own femininity. She could barely manage to appreciate another genuine human male these days, so strongly had this polarizing affected her. And though her brain-half maintained a slightly different hormone balance due to implants, it was far from effective. It was *easy* now, out on the streets, to catch sight of a pretty girl and feel the same exhilaration that coursed through the rest of the Tyler-body at Joe's instinctive insistence—if instinct was what it was. Or, she thought muddily, was that part guided by the cerebellum, or the midbrain, or . . . well, was it Benjy? Must be a loop. Reinforcing each other. And then she began picking up the loop too, was that it?

She felt dizzy, and realized they were moving slowly and deliberately out of the bank now. Had there been another flash of that necklace of insanely glimmering *monstro*sities?—and the underscoring of her accidental pun had been Joe's; shakily she grasped the fact that their minds were now linked, closely linked. Dizzy . . .

Sorry to take over so suddenly, Joe thought apologetically. But you were getting sort of rocky, swaying a little bit, with that . . . that picture of the generators, and I thought it was the simplest thing. You can have the carcass back as soon as you're feeling better; just ask, so we don't go offstride. We don't mesh so well these days; gotta be more careful. . . .

Her mind, her attention, slid away into restful blankness for a time; and when she came back to direct awareness, Tylerbody was sitting down in Parker's small apartment over the East River.

". . . easy enough for me to find work," Parker was saying. "I don't think Kinsolving's vindictive; but he couldn't stand the thought of me being punched onto one of his payroll tapes. Judging from what you've said, you're . . . not so well off. Which doesn't mean there aren't alternatives open to you. I've been checking into that. But you're going to have to keep an open mind."

"Give it straight," Joe was saying, and Jailyn realized her attention was still sliding away from all the words, words, words.

"Disappearances," Parker said. "I've been trying to track down brain-transplant subjects. Now, I expected them to be a bit tricky to locate. Privacy—you know it far better than I do!—seems to be important to transplantees.

"So when I couldn't locate any right off, it didn't bother me. I dug deeper. And I still couldn't find any.

"But I found trails.

"They seemed to lead to the country. Why, I don't know. But none appear to have returned. I know enough about the country to know it's not dangerous; and it may be that somehow they have some answers. I don't know. What do you think? For that matter, what do you know?"

Parker smiled, sat back, sipped at a drink.

"Never thought much about the country. Bunch of people out there wasting time when there are things to be done, I guess that's about the way I look at it. Like everyone else.

"Oh, I had a fling with the mind drugs when I was, oh, latter part of college, it was. Didn't do much for me; made me feel sort of . . . sort of just generally shitty, if you don't mind my putting it that way. But I read up on it a bit, later. Probably I wasn't ready, the books said—country propaganda—but I didn't really care, you know. I decided the whole thing didn't sound worth it. Kimmel, Tom Kimmel, his name was—my roommate at NYU North, a countryboy. Decent enough, I guess. But the multiwave was a lot more interesting than going off into the wilderness and, well, growing my own food and whatever they do, living, well, like animals, I suppose. I decided I was good enough to make a good multiwave man, enough to advance man's knowledge, and help him along the way to space, and all that. I dunno."

Hi. Joe shot at Jailyn. Glad to see you awake again —been following this?

"Like I said," Joe continued, "I never thought that much about the country; but I guess I've got a lot of ideas about it just the same."

Can I take over a bit?

My guest.

"The country always scared *me*," Jailyn said.

Parker recognized her intonations, and brightened.

"But I guess it wouldn't bother me that much, after all I've . . . we've . . . been through. And if other transplantees have gone there . . .

"I used to think it was awful, you know!" She giggled. "All those hairy messy people out there all paying no attention to the important things going on in the cities, in space. But that was the puzzling thing, you know—I met country people out in space! Puffing away at one of those maniacally carved pipes, or taking little pills every now and then, and spending all their time looking out viewports—not watching the screens, actually going to the hull and looking out through the glass. Strange . . . Still, I knew what they meant, just the same; I never got the feel of space myself until I was out alone in a suit. The dark side of Iapetus, it was. . . ." Her thoughts trailed off into memories of infinitely colored stars scattered everywhere on the black everythingness of space.

We should work on sidebands more often; that was pretty kicky!

A flash-glimpse of her Martian castle jumped into her mind and across to his without conscious direction: it was a night scene, and the castle loomed above them, thrusting up against the stars in their wild pure scatter across the alien heavens, blacker and clearer than from Earth though not as clear as space itself.

Then the thought was over and a great wash of nameless regrets swept irresistibly over Jailyn, and Tylerbody wept for a moment till they both made it take a breath.

Whew! I can't take much of that; talking about nonverbal communication . . . !

"Where was your roommate from?" Parker asked gently, after a moment. "Could you get in touch with him?"

Joe brought himself back with an effort. "Ohio, it was; some place between Columbus and Cleveland. I could find him, I suppose—have to go there, though. I don't know how else to get in touch with someone like that."

Parker nodded. "I think that's your best bet, then; you'll be safe enough in the country, and it's an off-beat idea—you probably won't have Kinsolving to deal with. And you might learn something."

"Do we have a choice?" Jailyn asked bitterly, and Joe answered immediately, "No."

And again Parker nodded.

CHAPTER ELEVEN

It had not been easy for Joe to find out how to get where he was going, even after he remembered the name of the old town near the Kimmel farm. Jailyn had lost track; they had gone to Cleveland, and then . . .

Transportation existed, but where? Just asking bearded people on the streets didn't serve, though country people did come to the cities frequently enough. Hair hadn't been a distinguishing feature for twenty-some years—the third major wave of hair growing in the country's history, as Jailyn had stated to Joe with some amusement.

Finally someone had directed them to a small lot on the southern outskirts of the city. Like most smaller cities, Cleveland was slowly but steadily losing population to the larger ones—and to the country, Jailyn and Joe both suspected, though figures on this were not publicly discussed with any enthusiasm.

They had taken an old noisy overstrip that brought them well past the spot they were supposed to get off at, before they realized it; a mile walk, all in all.

The sector of town they'd been deposited in was almost entirely deserted. The empty buildings around them as they walked seemed to stare at them with broken-window eyes.

From time to time they were startled to hear sounds of falling metal and bricks. Then they heard high-pitched laughter after a nearby "crash"—and around the next corner came a half dozen youngsters, laughing and running and leaping and looking back.

Country?

Townies, I'd bet a thousand. Sins of the fathers, being visited on the fathers' works by their sons; my, aren't we bitter? Tearing down what was built up at such cost to . . .

Tylerbody made an unnecessary gesture with left hand; the movement caught the attention of the group of vandals.

Well, it's why I found it so difficult—my Earth room in the castle.

He sent a cautioning thought at her, and she realized the townie vandals were coming closer, curious, investigating; very like a pack of wild animals checking over some new breed.

I'm probably better at coordinating the body, Jailyn, Joe thought after watching them a few moments longer. **At least for things like this. You'd better let me have full control. We'll need all the edge we can get, if . . . Well, there won't be anyone around helping us, that's sure.**

We're not that far from the airbus lot, from what that fellow told us, she protested.

Maybe not, Joe retorted testily, settling with some difficulty into full control of Tylerbody, **but they're between us and the lot. And, look, I don't know whether I can outfight them or not, but I'm very sure I can't outrun them.**

BENJY RUN NOW? BENJY LIKE TO RUN! BENJY RUN RUN RUN ALL THE TIME TILL FRIENDPEOPLE CAME HERE. BENJY RUN NOW?

No, Benjy, I don't think so, not just yet. We may have to fight a little before we run.

BENJY NO LIKE FIGHT.

Joe blinked. His lower lip had just been thrust out petulantly.

There's no time to argue, Benjy. Those are bad boys, and they're going to try to hurt us. We can't outrun them so we'll have to fight—

BENJY NOT LIKE TO HURT PEOPLE. BUT BENJY NOT LIKE BEING HURT. BENJY FIGHT IF YOU SAY WE HURT OTHERWISE. WHY CAN'T WE RUN?

That's a good Benjy, Jailyn thought abstractedly, knowing she was sounding foolish; but her attention was centered on observing Joe as he prepared them for the confrontation. *We can't run as fast these days as you used to, Benjy.*

The half dozen came nearer; some spread out onto the street.

On the other side of the street, abreast of them, a building wall had toppled over halfway out onto the roadway. The townie farthest out into the street turned his attention to the rubble, searching for a hunk of something to use in the impending attack.

To Joe the situation was obvious, and it was getting obvious to Jailyn: the six townie kids were determined to get some fun out of the intruder. He was big, but there were six of them. The youngest of them might have been twelve, the one searching for a brick. The oldest was perhaps sixteen; he stood directly in front of the Tylerbody and only a few paces away now.

"Will you let us pass?" Joe asked, knowing the question was useless but having to say something.

"Yaaaa," said the oldest conversationally, and stuck out his tongue. "Pay toll."

"What's the toll."

"You cry, we laugh!"

And the oldest leaped for him, while the others circled in closer and the one at the rubble picked up and hefted a brick in either hand.

Don't worry, Joe shot at Jailyn a moment after the lad closed with him. *He doesn't really know how to* fight—so the rest won't either, or one of them would've taken over already. This should be quick.

And quick it was.

The first boy found the sturdy twenty-year-old had slipped aside and had somehow propelled him with redoubled speed so quickly down the street that he could not keep his footing. The boy fell heavily onto the pavement, the wind knocked out of him.

The others hesitated, then two made for the stranger simultaneously. Joe ducked and hit one a solid blow in the stomach, causing him to double over on the spot and throw up on the sidewalk. The other was twisted around and held by the arms from behind, facing his fellows, before he realized what was happening.

The urchin at the rubble paused, still hefting the two bricks.

"Put 'em down," Joe made the Tylervoice say with all the menace he could command. "I'm no pedestrian, I'm an agent of Interfed. I'd just as soon kill all of you, and they'd give me a medal—if anybody gave a damn about you, which they don't. Now. Am I going to have to kill you all? I can do it with my bare hands, if you'd prefer. Or I have knives in my shoetips, if that sounds better. Then there are other things I could use —but I won't tell you what they are, because if I did I'd *have* to kill you. But if you're not off this street down that way—" he pointed back the way he had come "—in less than a minute, I *will* tell you. Then I'll kill you. What'll it be?"

"Jesus," muttered the frantically struggling kid he was holding. "Lemme go, huh? We'll clear out. We . . . we don't want no trouble with . . . with Interfeds." The boy swallowed nervously.

"You others first," Joe said, still quietly but with cold danger and menace in his voice. "Then I'll let this one go. And if I see you again, it's zzzzt!"

He could see eyes widen. He'd made the sound of the feared—and quite illegal—disrupter.

Now they wanted desperately to leave. No one wanted to be near a disrupter, or even near a man who would admit having one, for just the reason Joe had indicated —they wouldn't be safe with such knowledge, and they knew it.

They broke and ran; after a few seconds he slightly loosened his grip on the one he still held. This one immediately struggled even more desperately to break free.

"You. Listen, now," Joe hissed. "I've a mind to kill you just for a warning to your stupid friends, but I've got other things to do. So you get out of here with them, and get out fast, understand? And take your fearless leader with you."

He let go the boy's arms and stepped back at the same time, aiming and planting a solid kick on the boy's rear end—not nearly as heavily as it looked or as the terrified terrorizer felt it.

The boy started to run, then stopped for a moment by the sixteen-year-old, who had managed to get to his feet by this time. They whispered urgently for a couple of seconds, then the older one shot a horrified look at Joe.

Together the two began running down the street after the rest of their gang.

Whew! Thanks for not coming in with a scolding or a wisecrack about that line of crap I fed them!

Don't apologize!

BENJY RUN NOW? FUNNY FIGHT.

No run, Benjy. We don't need to. And isn't funny fighting a lot easier than real fighting?

Tylerbody grinned.

FUNNY FIGHTING OK, NOT SO MUCH WORK. BUT MAYBE NOT SO MUCH FUN. ALL WORDS. BENJY NOT UNDERSTAND WORDS BUT UNDERSTAND THOUGHT, YES? BENJY WANT TO RUN NOW.

So they ran, all the way to the airbus stop, and when they got there, the old man in the little cubicle near a dilapidated airbus didn't blink an eye at them. They laughed inside and didn't worry, and they got on the bus after the man assured them it was the one they wanted.

It was almost an hour before the airbus was ready to go, twenty passengers half-filling it. They were an oddly assorted lot, to the eye; no two were dressed alike, and their styles ran all the way from tatters to quiet elegance.

"Anybody mind some music?" someone called from the back, and presently a harmonica started up a simple tune.

After a few minutes the player went into another melody, this one more complex; he was immediately joined by a man sitting near the Tylerbody. This man was dressed as conservatively as an off-duty policeman, but he brought out a small, very ancient-looking banjo and began working it over expertly.

A pretty girl up front began singing words to the new tune, and presently someone joined in with harmony. Neither Joe nor Jailyn had ever heard the song before; it was soft, and arhythmic in the melody.

> "Going out, coming in,
> song, shout, spin, and grin;
> home is here, home is there,
> home the end where we begin.
> Going in, coming out,
> One time there, tomorrow was here;
> one time here, tomorrow was there. . . ."

It went on for some time much like that, and the first time through it made no sense to Tylerbody ears. It was done as a round, though part of it seemed to keep going with new words; someone always seemed to be picking up the old words, dropping into the song whenever beat and melody were reasonably close. It didn't seem to make any difference; it was a happy song and a light one, dropping into slow sadness; a singer or a player picked up the main thread of it for a while, perhaps to modify it into a minor key, repeat a fragment of it, over and over, or occasionally to do a more spectacular takeoff from it.

The bus made three stops before enough people had left that the song petered out naturally of its own accord. Joe checked the time absently—it had been over an hour.

They really keep at it, don't they?

I liked it. Wow! I don't understand how they all knew it, though. I mean, these aren't all country people, are they?

I didn't think so at first, but I guess they are. Somehow I'm getting the feeling country people know a little more about us than we do about them, you know?

Did you notice—people have been getting off, but almost nobody's getting on!

Frankly, I don't think anybody out here bothers to move around that much once they're where they want to be—unless it's going back to the city. Don't ask me why.

Huh. Cogent analysis.

Sorry; know little, talk much, I guess.

When they got off, an hour later, it was almost dusk. The airbus tilted and halted; the driver cut the fans down to idle while a short ramp extended out from the passenger section. A half dozen men and women in as many variations of ordinary work clothes got out first, followed slowly by the Tylerbody.

The airbus had pulled up at the top of a large hill overlooking what had once been a fairly large town—abandoned now for the most part, of course, like most other large country towns beyond the big-city limits.

Joe had spoken to the driver when they'd first started off. Now the driver told him, "Actually, I shoulda left you off a couple hundred yards back, but I thought you might like to see the view here. Sorta nice, eh?"

The half dozen who had preceded Tylerbody off the airbus had walked toward the edge of the hill and were now sitting there, past the disintegrating road now fit only for ground-effect transportation.

Shall we? Why not?

They walked toward the group at the verge of the steep hill, several hundred feet above the rotting roofs of the town that once began at the foot of the hill and spread out over most of the ground visible from the elevation.

In the dusk, however, there was not much to see, or so it seemed.

"It's good to take a look every now and then," someone said to them from nearby. One of those who had gotten off had wandered near the Tylerbody. "Kids ask about towns and cities every now and then. I like to know why I'm speaking against them, so I look. Mansfield, this one was called. Man's field? All those miles and miles of brick and concrete and ferroline? The stony civilization. Fields of . . . *made* things. Ahhh, I'm not a talker; I don't know how to word it.

"This was probably a nice enough place, anyway, but . . . well, time's gone past towns like this, all of them. People are either too rich or too poor to live here anymore, or just don't care, and I say it's a good thing. Though if you're not one of the folk, and you don't look as if you are, you'd put 'rich and poor' head-to-foot to how I meant it. But that's all right too."

Jailyn, is this kind of gabble the rustic wisdom we've come looking for?

Shut up and listen; you might find something out. Here, let me talk—

"We're—"

Jailyn broke off immediately, with the pronoun slip, then decided it made no difference. But she rephrased when she restarted. "I'm here to . . . drop in at the

Kimmel place. Knew Tom back in college. You're right, I'm not . . . one of the folk; but I'm here to . . . well, to listen to them, if they'll talk to me."

The man nodded as if it happened every day. "It happens every day," he said. "People come here to listen. Not right *here*, necessarily, but all the places like this. Not many, not enough to please me, maybe, but always a few. Some stay, some go back. And kids, kids are always coming to stay. 'Course," and the man chuckled, "*our* kids get footloose too, time to time; but city folk never realize we got our problems too!"

He laughed. " 'Course, the other side of that 'un is that most of ours come back—which mostly theirs never do! Too bad I didn't gather where you were bound, back on the bus, could've had a friendly chat. Mind if I walk there with you?"

Tylerbody eyebrows rose slightly, questioningly.

The man grinned. "I say that 'cause I got an interest at the Kimmel place, though I'm not part of the family. I wander more 'n most folk, so I've got interests several places; but now, well, I plan to settle in for a year or two. Might stay longer if the right Kimmel girl smiles at me! Come along, then," he said, and gestured back along broken asphalt the way the bus had come.

"They call me Prez, 'cause of my name, which is Pierce, Franklin Pierce. I figure I don't much look like my old namesake, but folks they call me Prez anyway. Come along, come along. It's dusk and dinnertime. Dusk and dinnertime," he repeated, pleased with the chance phrase.

He was nothing spectacular for their first conversation with a country man. Average height and build, plain clothes—real cloth by the look of wear on them. It was hard to tell his age; his face was lined only when he smiled.

The two male figures began walking.

"I was city-born myself," Prez said, "which accounts

for the name. But I set off for the country when I was fourteen. Northwest Territory, they nicknamed this part of the country, and it sounded good to me. Ended up at the Kimmels and they and me took to each other all right, so I stayed. Fifteen years ago that was, and I done some walkin' and some ridin' since then. Funny, though, allus come back to Kimmel's, when my feet get tired and my soul gets weary. Yeah," he said suddenly with a harder tone, "I know it sounds a little . . . silly, for a cityboy, talking like this. I'm not exactly folk myself, 'cause I never took the sacraments seriously and all. Well, hell," and now he was talking all in a rush, "that's why I come back this time. Figure it's about time I dug in and found out what's it about. Gettin' tired of kicking about."

What's he talking about, I wonder?

He may well be here for much the same reason we are.

Prez shot a glance at the Tylerbody. "I s'pose I shouldn't ask, but I'm wondering if you've come just curious, or are you thinkin' of staying?"

"I don't know," Joe said. "Maybe I've come to find out which."

Surprisingly, Prez nodded. " 'Bout what I said to myself fifteen years ago. Ha. Never did find out for sure. But all that's gonna change now; I been enough places, I guess. Like I said before, I'm not a talker; it's hard for me to word it. I gabble and I know it. But, well, here I am, ready to do whatever comes next. They never held me from walking away. Old Kimmel said I could go and come as I liked; 'course, anybody could come and go as he liked, but I knew what he meant, that it was ok, it was *allowed*, if you know what I mean?"

"Not really," Jailyn said, "but I'm learning."

"Yeah, well, like in the cities, there are so many things aren't allowed, you know. Inside and outside of you, if you know what I mean. This way to think, that way to act, traffic, people to watch out for, millions of people—it's just too much. Out here, you're *allowed*. Now, then, look at that!" Prez pointed off the broken highway as he finished speaking.

A narrow winding dirt road led away to the south of the main highway; back behind a stand of buckeyes, they could see lights—many dozens of lights, with more springing up even as they watched.

"Kimmel's," Prez said. "Lighting the lanterns against the dark."

"How many people are there, anyway?" Joe asked, and Prez cocked an eye at the change in the Tyler-voice.

"Fifty, maybe sixty," Prez answered. "Depends. It changes, you know. I'm not the only one as comes and goes.

"Most of 'em, when they go, they walk. Walk away, that's the way to leave, my friend; walking. Then you know you're doing something serious. And sometimes serious enough so that you realize you don't really want to leave, not just yet. And so you come right back.

"But when you do walk away, across the country, and do whatever you do when you get wherever you end up, and then you get tired and want to come back, then you take the fanbus. Coming back, you always seem to be in a hurry. Even the old folk, the wise ones, they walk away, and ride back, most of 'em, except for the holiest. For them it's always feet. But then, that's ok too."

Prez grinned as they turned down the road, and did a little dance step. Then he brought out a harmonica and began the "Going out, coming in" tune, and danced down the road ahead of them. His happiness at coming home was infectious; Joe and Jailyn both found themselves running to catch up to him, and laughing with the laughter that rolled out so easily around him.

"Hey, wow, it's Prez!" A boy about ten dropped out

of a buckeye in front of them, and danced around Prez
a few times. "Bring anything?" he asked breathlessly,
eyeing the large rucksack on Prez's back.

"Yes, oh yes," Prez said, still laughing, and made
the harmonica match his tones. "But that's for after-
dinner time, and story time, and such. It's no fair if
you know ahead what's coming."

"Aw," the boy said, "that's no fun!" But he didn't
seem downcast.

"Besides," Prez went on, all mock-parental of a
sudden, "it's dusk and dinnertime, and you're still
outside? It's me questioning you, m'lad, why you're
out here when there's chores inside for supper, eh?"

"Aw, chores," the boy said disgustedly. "Who needs
'em? Besides, they didn't call but once this time, and
I don't have to come till they call twice."

"Well, this is twice," Prez retorted cheerfully.
"There's always chores to be done, m'lad, so you might
as well do them when they come round. Else they'll
still be standing there, looking mournful at you, when
you'd *really* rather be doing something else—like listening to travelers' tales after dinner, and playin' the
piano like a showoff at the singin', huh?"

"Aw, chores," the boy said again; but his tone was
not resentful.

"Come along with us, now," Prez said. "We're going
up to the door straightaway, and you can slip inside
while we're introducin' on the steps."

"Who're you?" the boy said to Tylerbody.

"Come along," Prez said, his voice with a little edge
now, "and don't ask straight-out, it's not the way.
There'll be introductions and talk, don't worry. The
lad's got more energy than's good for any two," Prez
said to the tall figure dimly seen beside him in the
darkness.

Night had come, and even with the lanterns ahead
through the trees, it was no longer easy to follow
expressions, with moving leaf shadows dappling faces.

They came to the stand of buckeyes, and passed under them, and the broad, deep porch of a large three-story farmhouse was spread out in front of them. A myriad lanterns of all sizes, shapes, and colors hung from roof seas of nesting covering the underside of the porch roof.

The boy darted ahead and threw open the screen door, then the front door at the back of the huge porch. "Guests!" he shouted, as he disappeared inside, and the doors swinging shut cut off whatever else he might have said.

"Old Kimmel should be out in a minute," Prez said with great satisfaction. "Knew a grandson of his in college, you said?"

"Yes; Tom. Up at the Bronx NYU North Campus."

Prez nodded. "Once he came back, I never heard as he set foot more'n ten miles from here. He should be glad to see an old friend come from the shores of the ocean itself!"

"Well," Joe said hesistantly, "part of that might just turn out to be a problem."

The great front door opened slowly, just as the two men stepped up onto the porch. A tall stooped old man pushed open the screen door, and peered at them through horn-rimmed spectacles.

"Reverence, Grandfather," Prez said. "Franklin Pierce, come for a bit of sharin', if—"

"No ifs, Prez," the old man said, his voice strong and hearty. Then he straightened himself up as much as he could while the two visitors neared the doorway. "Are you leaving, or coming?"

"Coming, Grandfather. At least that's what I think I'm—"

"You are welcome to enter, boy." He stepped aside for Prez, who entered the farmhouse. It was obviously a custom, and not entirely rote, since Kimmel did not step aside until he had quite finished.

Then the old man turned to the Tylerbody, and peered for a long moment.

Then he shook himself slightly. "Forgive an old man's idle curious eye," he said. "Are you leaving, or coming?"

"I . . . I don't know what that means," Joe said, and felt like a foolish schoolboy asked for the second half of the alphabet when he has only troubled himself to learn the first half.

"Are you here," the old man said patiently, "because you are leaving another place, or are you here because this is the place you are coming to?"

Tylerbody grinned sheepishly. "Put that way, I guess it's simple enough: a little of both. I certainly left New York, though I'd sooner never have gone there of my own choice. But I was coming here, too. Uh, your grandson Tom, I . . . roomed with him in college. He . . . and he may not recognize me."

And *there* is one of the understatements of the decade, Joe thought at Jailyn.

But not the record. After all, there've been plenty of transplants coming to the country, if Parker's right.

"Jay may not, but I believe I do," the old man said. He stepped aside from the door. "And all three of you are welcome to step on in and share a little."

CHAPTER TWELVE

"I DO A LITTLE keeping track of city matters, though not all of my folks seem to understand why," Kimmel said, sitting back and lighting up a pipe. "And—in case you're wondering!—this here is tobacco." He grinned and blew a smoke ring.

Dinner was over; Kimmel had then led the Tylerbody up two flights of solid oaken stairs to his private quarters, which were large, plain, and comfortable—satisfying, like the meal they had just eaten.

Supper had been at a table huge enough for more than forty, though only twenty-three were present this particular evening. While women brought mountains of food in from the kitchen, they sang songs—astonishing Jailyn and Joe—and then fell silent to a low chant intoned by Kimmel, the words to which were obviously deep ritual, and which they as strangers found almost impossible to follow.

Talk at supper had been intermittent, inconsequential: plantings and reapings, the land and the things on the land, rather than the ebb and flow of personality conflicts usual in city gatherings.

Tom had not recognized the Tylerbody, nor did old Kimmel do anything to indicate there was any relationship between this stranger and Joe Winslow of NYU North.

"This here's Tyler," Kimmel said as they entered the kitchen where the rest of the family was gathering. "He's not folk, but he's a friend, and he's welcome to our sharing."

Then there had been introductions; Joe took the cue and said nothing special to Tom when they stuck out their hands to each other.

Over dessert, fresh ice cream and tiny sweet melons, it seemed to Joe that most of them had an expectant manner, as if it were time for Tyler to chat a little about himself. But old Kimmel was saying nothing and paying no attention, so Joe kept careful silence.

It's like old threedees, isn't it? The Old West back when people lived in all the little towns everywhere and rode around in gas buggies.

You're right—I mean, I thought country people, well, spent their time doing just terrible things, all full of sex and stupefaction and . . . and . . .

Maybe they do it, only just part-time. Look here, they obviously grow all their own food—at least it's a lot better than the mechanized-farm stuff we get in the cities—and they must have to spend a fair amount of time on that. And all that talk about bringing in hay, and all, just as if they were only farmers . . . I dunno; I'm gonna wait and see.

And presently the family began breaking away from the dinner table in small groups.

"Tyler and me, we're going upstairs a spell," old Kimmel said.

And then they were there, and the first thing Joe noticed was the threedee set, flush in the far wall.

"That's some of howcum I know who you are, lad," Kimmel said, seeing the surprised look. "Just because we're a ways away from what you folks are scurryin' about doing, doesn't mean we don't have someone keeping track. All kinds of trouble might be brewing. Me, I kinda like to keep on things anyway, though perhaps I should have better sense, especially at my age. Eighty-two," he added, cackling at the startled response.

Great God, I was sure he was sixty at the oldest, to look at him!

"If city people knew you had a fountain of youth out here," Joe said, "I think they'd all come to the country!"

Kimmel mock-scowled. "What'd we do with a bunch of city folk come down on us at once? No fountain of youth here, anyway; just working and living, and loving. Not a whole lot of worrying, though, not like city people. Do you like music?"

With this last, Kimmel turned away from them and fiddled with a pipe and a large pouch that had been sitting on the arm of a large overstuffed chair.

"Music?" Joe answered, bemused with the non sequitur. "Oh, music, yes, of course." He wondered if he should ask why, and decided he shouldn't.

But instead of commenting, Kimmel spoke of city matters, sat down, and announced, with amusement, he was smoking only tobacco.

"Tobacco?" Now Joe was too puzzled to keep from a question. "But I'd always heard . . . I mean, it isn't just illegal, it's bad for your health, isn't it? And yet you look—"

"Some people will always keep busy making some things illegal for a bunch of people who have a pretty good idea just what they're doing and feel they have a right to do it," Kimmel said in a breath, and his eyes twinkled with amusement at his own vehemence.

"You may not know it or believe it, or even care, but there was a time that all our holy sacraments were illegal, root and branch!" A wheezy cackle. "But laws against reality only last a certain time and then the laws are, well, I'd say transformed.

"Tobacco, now, it was legal a long time ago, but they decided—rightly enough—that cigarettes were makin' people all the time die of lung cancer and things.

Trouble is, they just went and made all tobacco against the law. Damn foolishness," he said without rancor, " 'cause a pipe after supper never hurt any man, and helped more than some live to a ripe old age in something like contentment. Like likker—which I admit ain't illegal, because they tried that once before.

"Likker, now, it's dangerous, real dangerous when you get the taste for it. But we all have a mug of stout now and then, out here, those that care to, dusk of a Saturday with work done for the week. Tch, lad, you have a shocked look on your face yet! Heh! Likely you'll get lots more shocks before you get used to the way things really are!"

And Kimmel sat back in his overstuffed chair and blew some more smoke rings.

"You mentioned music," Joe said, in desperation picking the first thought that crossed his mind.

"I did," said Kimmel. "Press that button on the desk there by you."

Joe looked around, and did so.

A broad expanse of plain paneling along one long wall immediately began rolling up out of sight.

Revealed were dozens of long rows of microtape reels.

"I got catalogs printed up on what I got," Kimmel said. "I expect it lists me havin' about 90 percent of the music that's ever been recorded, tucked away in there. I ain't got the only batch that large, of course; there's lots. And I ain't sayin' I ever listened to all of it, or even tried. A man can be wise, but he's still a man, and this man, he's got his likes and dislikes with music.

"Still, there's lots I like you might not think I would. What I like, it's printed in bold in the catalog. Heh, way you keep bogglin' at what I say, you're never going to make it through the night! Why, son, I've got tie-ins with the Yaletron; I can have that whole book completely reset with every word in it spelled backward, and get it printed, too, inside of fifteen seconds. 'Course, I don't, 'cause it would be wasteful. And expensive, though that don't matter as much as I suppose you'd think it does."

Joe took a catalog from a shelf by the microtape library, and carefully sat back down. Instead of looking at it, however, he found himself staring at the old man, who had picked up a well-worn copy of the catalog and was leafing through it, lips pursed.

I don't believe this old guy.

Joe! He's not lying, I'm sure of it.

No, no, I mean I don't believe *him*—I don't believe he's real! He's—he's more like some old college dean, retired and having his little jokes with innocent visitors. He can't be for real!

Kimmel was looking alertly at the Tylerbody now, peering over his archaic spectacles. "Well, now," he said, "let me get something peaceful playin' in the air. I've not been a good host. I've been talking as if you were only a visitor, and . . ."

But his voice trailed off just as Joe began taking an interest at last in what he was saying; and Kimmel began fiddling with controls revealed when he lifted gently on the arm of his chair. Then he punched in a code number, and a few seconds later Joe heard unfamiliar gentle music wafting through the room.

"Old stuff," Kimmel said with fairly obvious pride. "From the eighties. Beatles—the middle period. Oh, I know music's gone on a long way since back then, but that was when *I* was a kid, and to me there's never been anything like it. Why, the stuff they did in the eighties practically caused the Changes, singlehanded!"

"I prefer their later periods myself," Jailyn interposed, "but even the eighties stuff is better than modern music!"

"Ahhh," said Kimmel, "a man of discernment and— beg pardon, I detected a curious alteration in your voice pattern just then. Am I still addressing the same person? This *is* rather awkward; you know things *I* don't know, and yet I'm playing rather silly games with you, I perceive. Please forgive me." He made a gesture toward the dials.

"No, please leave it on," Jailyn said. "I'm Jailyn Rost and I like it. Up to now you've been talking to Joe Winslow."

Kimmel nodded. "Thank you for being patient with me, Miss Rost. I grow self-indulgent as my latter age grows upon me."

"It's all right," Joe said. "We've imposed on you just by coming here, especially since we don't even know whether you can—"

"Help you?" Kimmel sat back in his chair and blew some smoke rings toward his outstretched feet. One settled neatly round his upthrust left foot before dissipating, and he grinned. "Takes years to get control like that, and then it's half accident. Yes, I might be able to help you a little—help you help yourself, is the way it works.

"Now, I don't want to get into details this evening, but here's what I know about you, pretty much as it was given out. I know about your multiwave experience, Mr Winslow, though I know little about the multiwave itself. I know even more about your computer experience, Miss Rost, since I do know something about computers. That Yaletron tie-in, you know, and not by accident either. As for Benjy, if he's able to understand me, I'd like to tell him that he too is among friends now, who will cherish and support and love him as I am sure the two of you do."

BENJY SAYS NICE OLD MAN. LIKE . . . LIKE . . . LIKE MY . . . MY FATHER.

"Benjy says you remind him of his father, and he likes you," Jailyn said. "And he's never mentioned his father before. Of course, he doesn't exactly use words when he talks to us, but then, he doesn't have to."

Kimmel nodded and closed his eyes. "I followed the

earlier transplant cases. You may already know that
more than a few of them came to the country themselves, though none of them happened to come to this
part of Ohio. There was that uniform and curious
failure of their doctors to comprehend the lassitude, the
weariness, the spiritual depression that apparently
gripped them all sooner or later."

Jailyn started, and said, "Why, yes. But—"

Kimmel grinned, shaking his head in mock reproof.
"I keep telling you I'm on things, important things
at least. I could have told them how to keep those
transplants alive and sane, of course, but they wouldn't
have listened. They're all bound up in microhealing
and all that tricky, exacting work splicing up each nerve
just right, and all. Why, it surprises me they bother
to keep track of serotonin fluctuations. Sure they know
what to do—mechanically—but they didn't let you get
deep into each other's minds, did they? Kept your
minds pretty well isolated much of the time, right?
Antihysterics, antidepressants, numb-ers, neuroquench,
wall-offs, anything to keep you from really getting
inside things and seeing how they're put together.
Actually, I know why they do those things—*they're*
scared of what might get found out, not that they
suspect what it is."

"I really don't understand," Jailyn said, shaking
Tylerhead. "How you know all this, I mean. I thought
country people, well, went to the country for the simple
life, free of gadgets and all the, hm, trappings of
modern science. I mean . . ." She faltered, sensing
the confusion in her own mind and in her words.

"Of course you did," Kimmel said, then held up a
wrinkled hand. "Listen to this part building in the
music, now. Notice the stereophonics, the almost
fourth-dimensional effect, eh? Just listen. . . ."

Kimmel's voice drifted off and he leaned back in his
chair, shutting his eyes and smiling dreamily.

There must have been at least four speakers, Jailyn

thought. One at each corner of the wall of microtapes; no, there were four more, in the other corners of the room!

Sound now poured out on them in great thick layers: a deep three-dimensional layer that seemed to exist from the floor of the room up to their knees was a rich orchestral tapestry playing against the next layer, which felt like a dozen various percussion devices existing all about the room from their knees to above their heads. Above that there were instruments from other cultures, making plaintive sounds intermingling with three choruses of voices, layer on layer, bassos just above their head, baritones and mezzos next, and sopranos and tenors at the ceiling itself, all flowing together in profuse oriental carpets of sound, on and on and on, a paradigm of reality that left them all half awake, half in reverie by the time it was finished an endless time later. . . .

Wow! Joe sent at Jailyn after silence at last settled back in. *I never listened to that kind of music before!*

"It's not polite to keep our host in the dark," Jailyn said aloud.

"Oh," Joe said. "Uh, I never heard that before, Mr Kimmel, nothing like that at all. But music was never really my strong point. That . . . that was indescribable. And back in the *eighties?*"

"Yup," Kimmel said. "*Our* kind of music, of course, and it always was. People never really understood about that till it was too late. Joke was on them!" He laughed.

"What do you mean?"

"Oh, well, it's all tied in together," Kimmel answered. "A long lecture for an evening that's already turned late. But you might say the music was a first step, though it was more than that."

"But—"

"The music was ours, root and branch. But other people thought they could enjoy it—and they did.

And after they had enjoyed it for a while, they began
to become us, themselves. And after *that*, well . . .
that was when we got into the Changes."

"You know," Jailyn mused, "these days they just
teach that the Changes were part of the time of
troubles, like the plaguewars."

Kimmel nodded. "That's what they teach in the
cities; things have gotten back to their former—no,
that's a long, long story. You've traveled far and you
need rest. Be at peace here for a time. Oh; I believe
there is a Mr Kinsolving who is interested in your
whereabouts. Don't worry—if he can find you here
and get at you, he's far enough advanced that he
doesn't really need to."

"Advanced?" Jailyn said, weakly. "Do you know, I
am honestly not keeping up with this conversation!"

Kimmel got slowly to his feet. "My apologies once
more. I am speaking cryptically, where I should keep
silence. For tonight, my friends, let us carry to sleep
with us the memory of the music we have heard. A
room has been prepared for you—one of the younguns'll
show it to you."

Tylerbody rose, and Kimmel gave a call out the
door of his room.

A moment later a boy dashed in, younger than but
strongly resembling the one they'd met outside, with
Prez.

"Popo," Kimmel said, "I believe the guest room on
the third floor is ready for our guests—guest."

Popo didn't appear to notice the momentary slip of
tongue, but bobbed his head and said eagerly. "Yessir.
I'll show the way."

Kimmel rumpled the boy's tousled golden hair, then
shooed him out the door. Tylerbody followed; Joe
turned at the door.

"Thank you for your hospitality," Joe said. "It's
more than expected, really, and—"

"Never mind, never mind, have a good night's sleep.

We'll meet again for breakfast, eh? May God grant
you a restful night."

Tylerbody moved off after Popo, who darted away
and back as they made their way down the long hallway to the third-floor stairs.

Notice how he kept getting further and further
away from country speech, dropped in and out of
it? It doesn't upset me, but I think it's an interesting observation.

Mmmmm, Jailyn assented. *Jes' a poor ol' country
man—with a Yaletron computer hook up and one of the
largest microtape collections in the country. Tomorrow
I suppose we'll find he's one of the Secret Masters
of . . .*

The rest of her thought was stifled in a gigantic
Tylerbody yawn.

BENJY TIRED. SLEEP NOW. NICE MUSIC.

Their room was small but tidy, simple but satisfying
—and the bed was even more so. They were asleep,
the three of them, in minutes, deep restful sleep, rich
with dreams too deep to remember when they woke. . . .

CHAPTER THIRTEEN

"IF YOUR MIND runs in those directions," Kimmel said, "I suppose, yes, you could say I'm a kind of Secret Master. But I'm far from the only one." He shook his head and laughed.

The Tylerbody was stretched out at ease in a wicker rocking chair on the farmhouse front porch, while Kimmel sat—apparently comfortable—on a rug, cross-legged.

It was late morning. Warm breezes chased leaves across the porch, while out on the soft grass children played under buckeye trees. Women of the house, hanging clean clothes out to dry, kept an eye on the younger children as they played.

The men had gone out to the fields immediately after the breakfast Tylerbody had waked too late for; but one of the women had made breakfast specially for the late sleeper.

"But," Kimmel continued, "I don't have all the answers, oh, no, no, nor would I give them all, did I have them. As a for-instance of my fallibility, let us briefly touch once more on the slightly unhappy topic of Templeton Kinsolving. He is more tenacious and knowledgeable by far than I gave him credit for. He has already traced you to Cleveland—not a difficult task,

I should imagine, for I doubt you took sufficient care to protect your trail from hunters, eh?"

"No," Joe said, "and I don't really think that we could say either of us really knows how to."

Kimmel nodded. "It's an art form. However. When you made inquiries in Cleveland, how careful were you?"

"Well, I was smart enough not to mention the name Kimmel, or the place Mansfield. I asked for local transportation out of Cleveland to the country."

"Excellent," Kimmel said. "There are no little number of private transportation lines serving the folk, though I suspect the thought shocks you. Still, he has hired a Mr John Archer to find you, and my researches indicate that Mr Archer is no fool; therefore, Mr Kinsolving is not a fool."

"Archer?"

"Should you notice a very tall, very broad gentleman in your future travels, it may well be a skilled private detective name of Archer, yes, hm. By then it will be too late for evasive action—unless circumstances change. But do not worry, my friends. No one who makes himself known as an enemy sets foot anywhere on this land against our bidding. You are safe here."

Yet Kimmel belied his words by rising slowly to his feet, sitting down on another large overstuffed chair near the wicker rocker, and sighing and frowning.

"Nevertheless, there is now an element of haste which I must take into consideration. And haste can have a bad effect on judgment."

"Judgment as to what?" Joe asked.

"Whether you should take the soma, for the great journey through the world and your soul."

Tylerbody did not blink, but stood up and moved without conscious volition to the railing. Just then the sun broke from behind a small cloud, glaring full into Tylereyes.

Joe turned away blinking. "Soma? Huxley."

"Soma, yes," said Kimmel, "but not Huxley's. Forty years ago, when they discovered the Lost Vedas in the Cave of Babu Khazind in Nepal, they discovered jugs of soma seed—and about a third of the seeds were still fertile. Nobody was certain for thousands of years just what the soma of the Vedas had been. Now we use it for our sacred ritual drink; it is a true beverage of the gods.

"But truth is not to be cast into the wind, to be scattered about and lost. Soma is holy; we use it only on special occasions. And no one may take it save an initiate—which is where your problems begin to multiply, since you seem to be ignorant of the inner truths.

"You're built not to know them, of course. Repolarization's wiped out much of the effect of the Changes, in the last fifty years."

"Wait, now," said Jailyn, "you're as much a cause of this repolarization, living isolated in the country, keeping from the rest of us."

"In a way, perhaps. We came here as part of the Changes, and we've liked it well enough to stay. But we're also here because of farm automation—which feeds the cities and yet keeps enough land free for us to live comfortably on. I don't even mention hydroponics. How you can eat hydroponic food . . . Anyway, we're here, and to stay. What I meant was repolarization of attitudes. You don't realize it, but you're subtly taught to be afraid of us; and as a matter of fact we are a bit different—our germ-resistance pattern tends to be slightly skewed from city norms. You tend to get sick during cold-mutation onslaughts when we remain healthy, which is enough to spook anyone. Thing you don't realize is, we get hit by *other* cold mutations that never trouble you; you never bother to notice that, though.

"Why, you hardly know who we are! No wonder we're so distrusted! We're supposed to be the old revolutionaries, resigned to the simple life on the land, afraid—*afraid!*—to cope any longer with city life, and so forth. That's why there wasn't any revolution. Heh. But there were the Changes—and why? Because the changers changed the revolutionaries first, and when the plaguewars blew our way and killed more than half the population in just ten years, there were enough changers.

"So mankind stopped fighting wars. The plaguewars had solved India and China's overpopulation problems by killing 90 percent of them, plus a third of the rest of us. Peace. So science leaped forward at an even giddier pace, and city people turned back away from the Changes almost immediately. Space travel. This new multiwave. Think it'll turn out to be usable for faster-than-light travel, Joe?"

Surprised at the question, Joe shook Tylerhead. "Not a chance. Gravitation isn't a strong enough force—it's about the weakest one we know of. And the multiwave is only pseudogravitic—it uses a lot of energy, but all it produces is a very low gravity effect. We may some day learn how to modulate it for f-t-l communications; but that's another thing, entirely."

"And what will mankind do if the stars are unattainable, I wonder? Will they listen to us, at last?"

"What would you tell them?"

"Oh, many things, and many of them old. People should be let alone to do what they want, long as they don't keep someone else from what *he* wants. Let them grow, learn, change, live, and keep growing. It shouldn't be that difficult. But city life makes it hard to know what's really true; it's such an unnatural thing to begin with.

"But this is apart from your particular problem—since your accidents, I mean. Not all the scientific progress of the last sixty years has been true progress. Your operations, and the therapy afterward—all mechanical, all very intricately worked out, thoroughly monitored, checked every step of the way against charts, analyzed to the last observable detail. Planned. Mechanistic. Aimed to strengthen only the superego, if I may use a rather unsatisfactory substitute for a complex description of the error.

"Still, unknown to yourselves and to your doctors, you have done more than survive. That you both see three-dimensionally, that you both hear stereophonically, and that you touch, smell, and taste in common, and so forth, shows that you have unconsciously integrated most of the basic functions of your true natures.

"Indeed, you have in the past few months been living in a state of what, until your time, would have to be described as pure, constant telepathy.

"Most astonishing is that you don't yet realize what you've done! You think of yourselves as being in a kind of private war between the two of you—and yet you are almost at peace. Most of your nature has melded into a commonality of perception and function. You both only need realize this directly, and the wars that remain will be over!

"In fact, this is why you are here, though you're only discovering this fact now. This is why the others came to the country in the past, and others helped them to see."

"I think I'd better sit down again," Joe said, and dropped heavily into the wicker rocker.

"There are two ways to finally resolve your problem. One is to strengthen the concentration of your mind to the point that, perceiving suddenly with great clarity, you realize that in fact you have no problem. The other is through soma or, as you may find elsewhere in the country, its artificial cousins fashioned by man the clever ape. The difficulty with the first method, concentration, is that it may take half a decade or more. The difficulty with soma, among other things, is that you may encounter temporary delusions of a sufficiently convincing intensity as to falsely persuade you of their reality. This is the result of accelerating a natural process which, at its own pace, would present you with these delusions at a more leisurely rate, when your mind was naturally strong enough to withstand their temptations. With soma your mind may temporarily convince itself it has become seriously, perhaps permanently, aberrated.

"So we restrict soma, generally, to those who have been properly instructed in its use; and we do not use it frequently, though for social occasions and the like a very weak soma is brewed. It relaxes the mind and keys it up simultaneously, and is valued as an enhancement for entertainments." Kimmel cleared his throat and looked almost embarrassed. "Pardon me for sounding like a brochure, but there are certain things that you should have a clear understanding of."

Jailyn blinked, and realized she had not been following clearly the sense of Kimmel's words for some minutes.

Joe, do you—

Yeah. I do. Feel funny.

"Did you give us any of that soma with breakfast?" Joe asked. "Feel funny."

Kimmel frowned. "No, certainly not. No man has the right to force any modification of consciousness on another; and though that rule is bent perhaps more frequently than it should be, no, I would not do such a thing, nor permit it done. Hm. More likely, you're picking up somebody who is using it—though as this is a working day, I do not know who would be using soma . . . oh, yes, Prez. He's beginning his . . . final studies. Come to stay, no doubt of it. I can sense it now myself, though I am growing old and near the end of my time."

Jailyn shook Tylerhead, groggily. It was like the early days with Joe—disorientation. "And you say we're getting *less* insane? While you sit there talking about telepathy—"

"Which hasn't been studied in the cities since the plaguewars. First there wasn't time for such byways;

now they're far too hidebound again, more's the pity. But it's real, nonetheless, though it is not common. Frankly, it's not useful or practical, either. It's weak and it's chancy. We achieve it only seldom. But that you are sensitive to Prez tells me you have made far more progress than New Bellevue could ever understand."

"But . . . but I don't *like* it," Jailyn said, and Tyler-face made a momentary little-girl pout. "Can't you make it stop?"

Kimmel's voice had gotten softer, more distant. The sense of disorientation was sweeping over Jailyn now and she could barely make out what he was saying.

"It isn't happening to *you*, understand that. There are no unusual substances in your own system—you are only overhearing someone, what they're feeling rather than what they're saying. 'They' because there is a girl with him; they are working together. Consider also that the greater the intensity with which you receive such contacts, the closer you are, even now, before you have actually begun to do anything, to what you came here for."

"But I don't *know* why I came here," Jailyn wailed, in despair—and Joe laughed in her mind, and she listened to him laugh in her mind, and the despair shredded away into mist and she felt contentment, and then she began laughing.

Abruptly, however, the laughter stopped. "Why did I laugh?" she said. But she was no longer on the verge of hysteria.

"Undoubtedly Prez, or the girl, changed moods. Whereupon you stopped worrying because part of you realized suddenly that it was only a mood that was affecting you, after all. And it is in the nature of moods to come—and go. Insanity is only to attempt to hold onto one mood when another one comes upon you. That breaks the flow; that is incorrect."

Kimmel sucked on his pipe and observed the Tylerbody for some moments. "Flowing becomes difficult, also, when your superego is in tight control of what it thinks are conscious aspects of existence. Children everywhere know how to live every moment just as they go along; then children everywhere are taught, even here, to learn, to extend themselves into the past and into the future to gain such knowledge of the human condition as they can, to help them grow. And this changes them, breaks the flow, even here. Growing up in the cities you lose it almost altogether; here, we teach them to regain it when they are old enough to understand that they have lost it. Perhaps it is as simple as that."

"Simple?" Joe said.

"Simple in structure; the details are immensely complex. We're not fools, Joseph Winslow, nor were we during the plaguewars and the Changes. We are fully aware of the real world we all live in together. Here we work with nature—but we work also with knowledge. We work to gain food and clothing, to barter with —but we also work to create, both new knowledge and new beauty. We plant our gardens, and at the same time we are aware of the frontiers of knowledge and the mind, everywhere being pushed back exposing new territory. We know of the Red Spot Expedition, and about the second one that went looking for the first, and what they found. But who among you knows of Tanner's Synthesis or Lao Feng's work on dolphin communications? You gave up on dolphins forty years ago because you couldn't grasp the mode. But never mind about dolphins; it's enough you realize we too are involved in a kind of progress, though not in ways you'd recognize."

"You cover a lot of ground in a little time," Joe said. "It's a little difficult to follow."

"Not at all," Jailyn said. "I've gotten over whatever that was, and you're making perfect sense to me, sir."

"Each of us sees things through his own eyes first,"

Kimmel said dryly, "though such metaphors are risky with multiminds. It is similar to country and city; both use similar mechanical and organic devices and interpret the results of their actions. It is this interpretation that makes the difference between two or more societies, for each society finds its strength in a different interpretation. The country has its special strength in that we require nothing of our own people save that they be truly themselves, truly function as human beings, growing and learning and living in peace and joy. It is a simple concept, as I have said; but finally we have got it going. I do not expect you to accept what I say or its implications, just yet, but . . ."

"You don't expect us to believe you—but you feel sure that we soon will," Joe said, his tone not belligerent so much as puzzled.

"Words cannot convince you; you would have to live here for some time. And, as I said, I do not believe you will do so, at least in the near future; still, you will have made progress before you leave."

"It should be rather terrifying to hear you talk so calmly like that," Jailyn said. "How odd that it is not."

"What keeps you calm is that part of you recognizes I am only telling you what you already know; it's just that another part of you doesn't like to admit it's been found wrong.

"I used to tell the children who were starting to confront growing up, here, that what was causing them to imagine they were having this problem or that problem with the rather simple and straightforward task of growing up was their memory. More precisely, that part of their memory that is in charge, as it were, of locating particular memories on demand.

"Now, while you are awake, that memory-bank monitor is constantly keeping you up-to-date on what you see—telling you what's familiar, what's new; what's safe, what's dangerous; what's pleasant, what's unpleasant. The trouble is that the rest of the mind tends to accept what the memory-bank monitor tells it, while it's busy simultaneously feeding new information into the memory banks and receiving monitored judgments back on them.

"Because we're not supposed to be at the mercy of that memory-bank monitor. Somebody sets a mushy orange-colored food in front of you and your memory banks tell you the last time you ate food this color you got sick. When you're functioning properly, your—call it your creative intelligence for the time being—realizes that's not the whole story. This other part of your mind, in other words, goes to a different level of your memories on its own, and comes up with the fact that it was a rotten banana. Considering that the food now in front of you is a sectioned orange, you override your memory-bank monitor and eat the orange.

"Now let's say the orange is rotten too: the *next* time you get a serving of orange-colored glop you might find yourself seriously impeded in any rational attempt to eat it, even if you immediately recognize it for creamed tangerine.

"What happens after a number of incidents of this nature is that your memory-bank monitor gets the idea that it's *you*, so to speak. It gets conservative; it doesn't want to have to bother processing brand-new information all the time; it's easier to process familiar types of information. When it gets to the point where habit dictates a large percentage of your actions, you stop learning, slowly; you begin repeating old actions and old experiences not because they're pleasurable so much as because they're familiar. Familiarity doesn't strain your memory banks and the monitor. You get stodgy. You stop enjoying new things because new things are harder to file away. Life gets to be a matter of belated reactions to stimuli, and you limit the number of stimuli to as narrow a band as possible, even though you don't consciously realize that any of this is happening at all. Your memories come to think they

have become you, as if the burned match were the fire.
And thereby, eventually, you are trapped."

There was a low uneven whistle, then: "Benjy . . .
under-. . . stand," came a raw-voiced response from
Tylerthroat.

Benjy!

Kimmel cocked his head and stared into Tylereyes.
"Well, now. Remarkable. I take it this is an unusual
occurrence?"

Joe struggled to speak, aware that in the back of his
mind there was a running echo of whatever was going
through what was left of the mind of Benjy Tyler.
And right now the Benjymind seemed to be greatly
preoccupied with itself and in quiet pleased astonishment; at any rate, Benjy wasn't responding to Joe's
thoughts.

"You can say . . . that was an unusual occurrence
. . . yes," Joe finally got out.

"You use his body to survive—he has begun using
your minds to express himself. It is . . . encouraging."

Jailyn wanted to scream. Too much had happened.
They had lived together in the same skull, three of
them, running the same body by now so efficiently that
they hardly noticed. Either Joe or Jailyn could handle
the whole problem of conscious function, or interact
with the other when necessary.

It seemed simple that way—they even had their
memories in common, whenever they relaxed instinctive guard.

She tried again to contact Benjy, and then there
he was.

BENJY UNDERSTAND. BENJY HAPPY. BUT THINKING IS
HARD HARD WORK. I LISTEN MORE NOW.

As before, communication was not in words but in
half-sharpened thought concepts; now she could sense
Benjy's mind savoring them as sublime almost past expression or belief. She drew away and he returned to
blissful contemplation of the heights.

Kimmel got spryly to his feet. "I have decided. You may take the soma if you wish. I will say no more; words would only confuse you. You are capable of perceiving the truth, so I believe now; and I hope only that you will believe me."

"Then you think it is . . . safe, after all?" Jailyn said.

"You will be voyaging out onto the far seas of your mind," Kimmel answered. "You cannot drown, but for a time you might come to believe you can. And should it chance you come to think that you are dying, you may even choose to die. But it will be a death in the spirit only, and afterward there comes rebirth. I do not feel that you will achieve this on your first attempt, however."

"You have quite a sense of the anticlimax, sir," Joe said.

Kimmel smiled quietly. "As the saying has said, it goes with the territory."

"Unnerstand . . . anyclimax," said Benjy in a whisper of rasping Tylervoice.

Then he laughed in childish glee.

CHAPTER FOURTEEN

THE SOMA was almost without taste; bland; innocuous. Soft intricate music was playing as Tylerbody sat opposite Kimmel in the latter's room.

"How long does this stuff take to work?" Joe asked, wondering if his tongue was getting thick already.

"There are no absolute guidelines, but the tendency is for it to take about an hour. There are occasions when people gain the effect in spirit before they do in body, or so I like to phrase it. But this may be auto-suggestion. It may also relate to occasional ESP phenomena that are encountered. These last, by the way, can be dangerous distractions on the road to integrating your perceptions of the realities. However, I shall be here, so you need fear nothing."

"I fear nothing," said Jailyn, then withdrew to think about why she always said that, whether or not she knew it was true at the time.

"You talk different now," said the Benjywhisper to Kimmel.

"Yes," said Kimmel calmly, "I am a human being, and it suits me at times to act in such and such a fashion, at another time to act in another fashion. I allow my moods to exist in freedom—and I allow them to pass, making way for the next." He smiled. "There is something of a knack to it, I may tell you that.

Don't expect to understand the secret immediately. That could be an unfortunate mistake, insofar as it might cause you needless anxiety."

They sat in silence for a time, listening to the music, as Kimmel had suggested.

"You will probably keep your individual experiences and reactions to yourselves for a time," Kimmel observed finally. "During the experience, I mean. That goes whether you have positive or negative reactions; these being basically superego productions, they are individual to each of you and have no primary relevance to the other. More basic experiences will tend to be common to both of you."

"You know, I was wondering about that," Joe said, and smiled sheepishly.

They went back to the music. . . .

Jailyn became slowly aware that Joe was aware that they were both aware of each other and of Kimmel, and that simultaneously they both and separately were aware also of Benjy; and to a lesser extent Benjy was aware of them; and they were all perceiving the room and everything in it directly, wordlessly; and the music had expanded far beyond their minds, subtly coming to imply an entirely new universe of discourse far, far beyond her own old horizons. . . .

Joe struggled with his thoughts. . . . articulate the nature of this complexity of interrelated perceptions . . . all of which add up to nothing else than total perception of total reality . . .

But even as he struggled, the mood changed; and he perceived emotional tensions, radiating from his mind and from Jailyn's—instinctively he closed off his perception of her, tried to keep from touching her mind with his own proliferating thoughts.

Eyes, then . . . whose eyes? And . . . who is thinking of them? None of us, and three of us, and yet the eyes are there for all that. I do not understand. Is there anything to understand? Eyes see; eyes do not see without mind; there is no sound in the forest of a falling tree, if no ear has heard it.

Yet there was a vibration pattern set up in the air molecules, to be heard by any who would listen; was there not? Postulate: God exists because the world exists; the world's existence proves God's existence because nothing exists unless it is perceived; therefore God exists, perceiving everything that the rest of us do not.

I don't believe that.

He paused, aware he was struggling desperately with useless verbalizations, dimly aware that he was being gently seduced from his syllogisms.

He tried to analyze what he had just been thinking, and found he could not remember even the subject of his thoughts.

Then he found he could not think discrete thoughts about any of his perceptions any longer. He felt a twinge of fear that he was sinking into Benjy-mindlessness, and then remembered Kimmel's assurances and relaxed, and wondered that he was able to relax.

He began to feel as if his body was glowing subtly with new life, that the room and the music were glowing with life, that the entire world was glowing and pulsating with life and energy. . . .

And, of course, it is! came one drifting lonely gleeful separate thought.

Jailyn broke away from Joe's thoughts—which she found herself following absorbedly—when she realized he was trying to pull away from her.

She wondered briefly what had upset him. But there was no more time for wondering. Music was pouring over her in oceanic waves, inundating her with endless shifting tides of emotions and delights and tiny sorrows, flowing this way and that without her will and without her worry.

She became aware that she was not aware of certain things.

She could not feel the chair they were sitting in.

She did not feel the Tylerbody, except as if at the wrong end of a telescope. Her mind drew a lightning series of conclusions, until it ended up facing itself with a new wonderment. For she was first startled to realize that the Tylerbody penis was as distant as the rest of the body, which she realized was her body and not her body; and before she had time to more than briefly wonder if that perception was not really rather banal, the remainder of the thought caught up with her racing imagination.

The completed thought brought with it a wave of shuddering relief, for she saw that she knew she could endure, now, this Tylerbody existence, could live the rest of her life in a man's body, making the best of it.

I still live! she quoted to herself, and a thrill ran through and through and through her as she felt old dark terrors shred away, the cloud at the back of her mind disintegrating, and life was there with her to be lived.

Anxiety returned when she saw the lamp beside old Kimmel glow and expand and pulsate with an inner inexplicable life of its own, growing until it filled the room, twining itself into and through the onrushing music that still played softly on and on. But the music was getting fainter and fainter and the light was getting brighter and brighter and brighter until its pressure on her made her scream silently, while part of her still knew she only wanted to feel the light, feel it course through her and become her so that she herself could shine like the light and fill the world with glory and endless brilliant energy. . . .

Joe felt the texture of the Tylerbody palms against each other, and wondered once more at their strange softness, wondering at the same time how it was he was still sane when he was condemned—for a lifetime! —to manipulating another man's hands, another man's legs. . . . Sharing it, too, with others chosen at random by solar fates.

But the moment of strangeness passed, like a mood of a sharp strange smell one cannot recognize but which one decides to forget before it worries him; the smell perhaps remains, but does not obtrude, barring other symptoms such as those perhaps of poison gas. Poison gas? Texture strange so strange to him that the thought and the word and the reality and the reaction now all jumbled themselves together and seemed to be aspects of the same reality, whatever that was, whatever that was. . . .

Meanwhile Kimmel sat quietly, sucking on his old corncob though the mite of tobacco he'd allowed himself had long since gone out. The figure opposite him sagged back in full relaxation. Fleeting expressions had begun to chase across the boyish face immediately, touching it lightly and passing away.

There were many expressions, ordinarily a clear indication that the soma was going to precipitate the subject into less productive, overemotional experiences. But he did not worry; *After all,* he thought, *there are three of them using the one set of muscles.*

He did not worry; yet he was uneasy. He had never guided a transplant; no one had guided a double-transplant. There could be trouble; still, it was better to let them work through it than to try to alert them, and thereby possibly alarm them.

He continued to watch alertly, while the sleeping face, alive with shifting impressions, emotions, reactions, slowly became peaceful and serene as they drifted to deeper levels. . . .

Now she began to taste the flow of energy alive about her in the room, the universe, her, and she turned her attention inward—perceiving as she did a small young Benjy perceiving her with awe. An even deeper feeling of comfort and well-being slowly pervaded her mind and, yes, her body, yes, *hers*, and Benjy's body, yes . . . and it was all right that things were this way, for she could live and they could live. It was new and different but it was real; simple and not-simple both; a challenge to meet and grow with, just as Kimmel said.

She and Benjy caught breath simultaneously, tasting overtones of new harmony between them.

And then she turned her newly tuned perceptions back at last toward Joe, through strange mists between them, and saw trouble

Joe sank into nets of language logics weaving themselves in and through sharp new textures of common things he was somehow perceiving. At the same time slowly a light feeling of ultimate inchoate dread began to shadow a part of his mind, toward the back. He tried to wince at the effort not to concentrate on that shadowy shadow because he only wanted to relax, relax and know the release, relief, purging-joy sensation Kimmel had hinted of.

But the shadow was there and a fragment of an old old tale seemed to bob up in his mind and sink below again before he could pick it out of the murky seas of his mind where shadows grew in the southeast by mountains he had never seen before . . . a fear seemed to grow in him from nowhere and for the first time he thought that he might awaken, try to speak to Kimmel about this; but he could not so much as tense his vocal cords. Somehow Jailyn was newly strong and held the speechways, though she too was silent unseen by him, rapt in some long internal contemplation he shied hastily away from noticing. . . .

And now he was alone again, not even master of his

voice, his body—nor even of his mind, for even as he cast a despairing look backward the shadow had grown once more. It seemed now to be of a flavor with the disasters of the world that had never changed in spite of the Changes, the dreaded lives of emptiness stretching out through endless empty city streets where men refused to remember and women also and their children; refused to look inside and taste their minds that they could look outward once again with eyes and souls refreshed.

Language logic weaved other nets, heightened what he saw too clearly about what he had always thought he knew. For now he saw for the first time clearly that the Changes, indeed, had not lasted in the cities. Perhaps staying in the cities kept the poison of it circulating in the nervous system so that all sank back, back; it was hard to feel as he felt now with a hard chill certainty that rang like dull iron in his mind; it was hard to feel, to perceive that chill settling down once more over mankind. For space, after all, was not a wide frontier; the solar system was fated to contain mankind throughout its future; for over a century the wisest men had known this. And so few could travel, after all, even to Mars, and the moon colonies would never be large compared to Earth's population. . . .

He cursed silently as travel posters flared in his mind and census statistics reeled off, flow patterns, some abstractions from reality, some merely mimics of it, indicating stasis, mankind trapped in Earth's gravity well, their spirits trapped in the space-time well of the sun, never to reach out and reach life elsewhere but forever doomed to be alone, alone, alone, alone, alone, and there were no lensmen to save us from the great black dark out there. . . .

Was that the fragment? no . . . shadow growing, growing, what did I say? what was the phrase, what did they say, didn't someone throw that damned ring in the fire long ago? Into his awareness leaped a scene with strange scents and musics and an eternal dawn, and two figures stood near an elven boat and, "You fool! You were supposed to throw it in the *center* crack!"

He tried, tried, tried to laugh while Tylervoice croaked meaninglessly through the darkness now that was growing so great. "The crow!" he said aloud in his mind, and tried to laugh once more

—and was there now a great Eye piercing through the Darkness, looking straight at him?

From the serenely placid Tylerface broke suddenly a sharp, suddenly choked-off scream so filled with momentary horror so vast that Kimmel actually elbowed the microtaper's volume control in a ̶ ̶ ̶ ̶ ̶ ̶ ̶ "What's wrong?" he said, as soon as ̶ ̶ ̶ ̶ ̶ ̶ sudden blare of pure raw sound back down ̶ ̶ ̶ ̶ ̶ ity. "Are you both up and out, or just one?"

"Joe's scared badly," Jailyn said, not even astonished to find herself apparently awake and in control of herself, "but I'm ok. Talk to him. I don't know what happened, and he cut me off so sharply my head still aches."

"Joe," said Kimmel. "Joe. Everything's all right, do you understand? You are only seeing pictures in your mind. They are not real, they are not important, and most definitely they cannot hurt you."

"The Eye," Joe found himself gasping aloud; and even as he spoke the feeling of ultimate dread that had shot through him began to fade, as he realized what must have happened.

He breathed deeply, realizing that Jailyn had gracefully withdrawn again from any contact, unmistakably leaving him in control. He felt better—that she trusted him to recover and not to do them harm, that she understood instinctively what he understood only with difficulty, that he needed simply to feel in touch with reality, just for moments. The scare had been deep; yet they now seemed both to know, it had been heal-

ing; for the Eye, the great malefic Eye peering through
the Darkness (and he began chuckling now before he
could even find the words in his mind to explain it to
himself verbally), the Eye had only been Jailyn, wanting to help him, trying to make contact, and the Eye
wasn't real, it was only his own mind tricking him, and
he stopped laughing and smiled at Kimmel. . . .

"I read too much," Joe said to Kimmel conversationally, which took Kimmel slightly off guard; Joe
smiled at this. " 'The Downfall of the Lord of the
rings,' " he continued. "I felt alone and afraid, ready
to go down in defeat and despair; a really bitter mood.
And my mind translated it into a familiar story; so
then   Eye from Mordor at the back of my
very   and I tasted fear—and simultaneously
realiz   didn't exist, that fear, evil, don't really exist,
except when you think they do. And of course the Eye
vanished from my mind and it was Jailyn, only Jailyn,
looking to me with concern. Yet the Eye was only in
my mind, my own interpretation of . . . of her. Apparently my mind has offered me a metaphor of what
I have been fearing, so that I could dissipate it."

Kimmel nodded to him, smiling. "You have made
gains. But—if you will accept this only as a suggestion
—allow yourself to get in touch with Jailyn once more.
I believe she has made more progress than you. I believe the results will be good; but I warn you I cannot
predict what those results might be. This has been a
surprising time."

Joe frowned. "I'm still feeling shaky. And the soma
effects seem to have vanished completely."

Once more Kimmel nodded. "That too is temporary,
though it's a bit unusual that you have been able to
talk to me so coherently for so long at this stage. It
would seem your minds can handle new perceptions
far more quickly than I'd expected. Thus you stabilize
yourself, momentarily holding off the apparent effects
. . . but I verbalize, inexcusably. Your pardon. Let me

assure you that I now know that you are safe, quite
safe—safer now, I should imagine, than any novice has
a right to be!"

Joe closed Tylereyes, but opened them immediately
and sighed. He tried a smile. It seemed to work. He
felt good.

But then his body began to feel as if it were one
great smile, all smiling, and this inexplicable sensation
gave him a vast unsettling feeling of puzzlement, or
was it wonderment; and he was sinking into the wonderment and smile before he knew he was sinking, and
sank deep, deep, deep, and wondered for one last fleeting moment how he had managed only a moment ago
to shape words in his mind and actually attempt to
speak them to another man while the ▓▓▓▓ began
to tune up within him into his consciou▓ ▓▓▓ ▓▓▓
there was a great flood of light and inner ▓▓▓
titanic frames of mind, and there was Jailyn too and
the touch of her distant mind was comforting and he saw
Benjy in her mind with her and he felt a great current
sweep him out toward her mind and as they told it
later they were

together looking out of THEIR eyes at the room
alive with the dancing colors of the music and the
smell of its touch and the richly glowing flame that
was the old man and his pure bright clear mind flowing with the music as it danced the room and walls
and all the people in the farmhouse and THEY
breathed deeply and saw all the people in the farmhouse breathe deeply at the same time and THEY
blinked THEIR eyes and drew away from what THEY
were seeing and realized also that THEIR eyes had
never been open but that THEY had seen the people
in the farmhouse with THEIR mind as it flashed the
universe into creation over and over again instant by
instant and THEY sank back away from the house and
the room back into THEMSELVES and contemplated

that which was within, and together for a time THEY
stared in unity at the unity beyond sadness and joy
and were part of it and knew nothing whatsoever save
everything. . . .

And after a time THEY slid slowly off the large chair
onto the softly carpeted floor and said "oooooooooooooo
oooooooooooooo" and Kimmel came and knelt beside
THEM, calmly checking pulse and forehead and then
sitting on the floor cross-legged beside THEM and observing THEM closely but calmly, and read to himself
quietly out of an ancient book of comfort for a time
until THEY had come back swiftly up through the
bardos and lay there quietly looking up at him and
Kimmel said to THEM, "You can be anything you
want to be, anything that is possible is possible."

And THEY sighed and smiled and looked outward
once more after perceiving the common oneness between the three of THEM and THEY perceived Kimmel once more. His mind, directly tuned now to
THEIRS, was open so that THEY touched the surface
of his thoughts and he gave a great "Ahhhh" of surprise
and held his position, arms partly extended from his
body, and THEY saw Prez six rooms away splashing
water in his face and THEY touched his mind before
THEY knew it and Prez stopped with his hands halfway to a dry towel and THEY touched minds and
minds and minds until in THEIR mind THEIR picture of the farmhouse was ablaze with the presence of
other minds all touched and held for a timeless moment in a pure wordless strange communication like
cold flame, like a cube of ice made from fire, roaring
quietly, comfortably, in *all* their minds. THEY shuddered with inexpressible feelings as THEY felt THEIR
mind pass on beyond the farmhouse into the fields;
THEY felt the presence of the soft warm earth and
the growing things in the field and on the hillsides and
the men and the women and the children and their
minds, and THEY touched them all for that endless

moment. And then THEY saw the sun though THEIR eyes were closed and THEY were closed about in a small room and the sun roared with quiet power and Joe felt the long slow beat of the waves of gravity throbbing now and ever through the vastnesses of ultimate space and holding Earth in her course and the planets and Joe felt their presence and their gravity while Jailyn touched minds on Earth and then he was back with her again and THEIR mind with Benjy's reached out and saw glowing dots throughout the center of the continent, minds of others like Kimmel and those on Kimmel's lands, their lands, and they all felt THEM as THEY reached the limit of THEIR strength to touch, to hold to other minds; and the contacts fell away. And THEY were once more alone except for Kimmel, who now dropped his ▮▮▮ into his lap and with straight back and eyes lowered ▮▮ breathing calmly and slowly, calming and slowing THEM by his calm balanced presence.

And THEY went out again with Joe and saw the sun and the moon and the eight worlds each alive with the long slow beat of their mass propagating at irregular swirling rates and Joe sank back quickly into THEM and THEY looked calmly on the moiling energies that swept through the solar system and THEY saw little winking points of pseudomass, Monstro and other great fish of the man-sea, the multiwave generators scattered throughout the system in the myriad groping useless tests, for THEY now perceived the harmonics of the sun and the moon and the planets resonating with the music of the heavens, and sank back away onto the carpet in front of Kimmel and

Jailyn said weakly, "How much more can we take?"

And Kimmel said, "You are here and may do as you like," and Jailyn giggled and then Joe cleared Tylerthroat and Benjy floated in blisses beyond his imagination, and THEY looked within for a moment and THEY knew that it would be well to stop now, and Jailyn said, "Hi!"

and Joe said, "I guess we're back,"

and Benjy whispered, "What happened?"

and Kimmel said, "You tell me."

And, slowly, hesitatingly, some of it THEY did tell him, and marveled that the memory did not fade away like some fragile dream swept clean away by sharp morning breezes, and THEY returned into each other and felt happy for a time,

and Kimmel said, "Perhaps now you should sleep for a time,"

and right there on the soft warm carpet with soft warm music comforting THEM, THEY fell asleep together and dreamed dreams THEY could hardly bear to remember for the rest of THEIR lives. . . .

CHAPTER FIFTEEN

"MINDTOUCH IS RARE," said Kimmel.

"I'll just bet it is," Joe said.

Once more they sat on the front porch of the Kimmel farmhouse. The late afternoon sun cast merry dappled shadows through the trees. When men and women came onto the porch, all would silently wave to all; no more words of greeting were necessary.

"Mindtouch, in fact, has almost no place in our scheme of things," Kimmel went on imperturbably. "As with the ability to predict the future, or the utilization of any of the possible varieties of telekinetic power. We disregard them, as wise men have always disregarded such impediments on the way to truth. At least, we disregard them as long as we are still searching within ourselves. Not only that, it now seems certain that such esper phenomena are inherently weak forces —just as gravitation is weak. Yes, of course, I realize the multiwave is considered to be a mechanically propagated pseudogravitic phenomenon, but look at the power it takes, just to obtain what is really a very minor effect. Too much power, if it weren't for controlled plasma fusion. . . ."

Jailyn wrinkled Tylerbrow. "Very well, the esper

power may be real, but it's weak and unimportant. I can accept that."

"Because it's weak, mindtouches seldom occur. It makes no fundamental difference that we out here are more generally knowledgeable in the inner workings of the mind; human brains are really capable of generating only a minuscule amount of power. Electrochemical systems acting only with organic substances, within a prison of bone—well, it is not so surprising the brain can so seldom reach outside itself.

"However. With you I am presented yet another conundrum, of sorts. You managed to establish momentarily a wider-ranging mindtouch than we were prepared for. It may be a factor of the subtle differences in ESP potential between your three minds; it may be the result of the fact that you three are already in virtual telepathic communication. I am inclined to the latter supposition; at any rate, it will provide food for analysis for many years to come. You have brought us a gift of new knowledge; we are in your debt."

"Frankly," said Jailyn with a laugh, "I'm not sure I understand anything about what happened. Am I supposed to?"

"There are some implications and lessons, perhaps." Kimmel sat back and blew a smoke ring. "You haven't been turned into adepts, for instance; you'd have much work indeed ahead of you if you decided on that direction. Second, you have produced some of the most spectacular side effects on record, which means, unfortunately, that you will probably have even more difficulty keeping to the inward road. Third, the time for the inward road, for you, is not yet; you have another path to tread."

"The multiwave," Joe said, nodding his head.

"What *about* the multiwave?" Jailyn asked immediately.

Tylerbody laughed with THEM a moment, for con-

versing aloud among THEMselves; yet Jailyn immediately stepped back from Joe's mind.

"The multiwave," Joe repeated, "I saw it." He spoke
simply, with the manner of one who has stated his
point so completely it needs no further explication.

"*We* saw it, you mean," Jailyn said. "And so what?
We saw many things—minds, too, and touched them.
We saw the sun's gravitational field, felt Earth's throbbing through our mind. We also experienced a number
of other fascinating perceptions. So why pick on the
multiwave?"

"We saw it," Joe said again. "And I think I understand it now. It's been there for weeks—months. Only
I didn't want to understand it. For us, it would be
quite simple, I think—if we were only there."

"There? Where?" Jailyn wished now she were touching his mind, but that stung, somehow. So she spoke
aloud.

"Why, there on Monstro," Joe answered.

"With the world opening up before us, you want
to pick up and flare away to some *asteroid?*" Jailyn was
genuinely astonished.

Kimmel was smiling gently, and now nodded. "Quite
possibly that is exactly what you should do. During
the mindtouch, I felt part of what Joe seems to be
talking about—and he's an expert multiwave technician.
You'd be enthusiastic, Miss Rost, if you had, say, directly perceived the consciousness of that Yaletron I
plug into from time to time. Wouldn't you be de-
lighted to get the chance to explore some of those
subtler mysteries of computer operation such an experience might give you?"

Jailyn wanted to shrug and sit back, but Joe made
Tylerbody sit far forward eagerly.

"Then you do understand," Joe exclaimed. "It's in
the harmonic tuning. Jailyn didn't grasp the implications, but I could tell. We can see the multiwave; if

we were on Monstro, I believe we could control it."
He didn't try to elaborate, but ideas were racing through
his mind now. "Of course," and his mood shifted instantly downward, "they'd have me strapped to the
table with the saws digging away at my prefrontal
lobes if I tried to tell, oh, Al Zink something like
that."

The screen door slammed and bare feet slapped
rapidly around the corner of the porch.

It was Prez.

"That Kinsolving's got good instincts in his hiring
—got a call that a man of Archer's description has been
seen poking around down in Old Mansfield. 'Course,
he won't find much out from whoever's still hanging
on there. But—how'd he know to be there in the first
place?"

Kimmel frowned. "The answer is that he should not
have."

"Those kids," Joe began.

"Hush," said Jailyn.

"No," Joe continued, "I won't hush. Archer may
have gotten in touch somehow with that gang in
Cleveland—aren't detectives supposed to know all the
scum? And just maybe, some of those kids had a grudge
on; maybe one or two sneaked after us, in spite of the
scare I tried to throw into them. Maybe they found out
where we were going . . ."

Kimmel looked worriedly at Tylerbody. "You are
probably right. You should have told me about this
incident—though I suppose I could have done nothing.
However, this does bring up a new problem. If Archer's
gotten this far, I cannot any longer be certain he'll
get no farther; he seems to be quite the thorough in-
vestigator. This may be a sign to you—for you to interpret by yourselves."

Joe rubbed hands on face. "I'm drained. Jailyn?"

"Yes," she said; then, to Kimmel and Prez, "strong

physical reactions. Catching up. We're exhausted. Wow, that comes on fast, when it comes!"

"I understand," Kimmel said. "Get some more sleep. Archer cannot get to you here to hurt you."

They slept for ten hours after the time of visions; now they slept till late morning, waking with unfocused memories of strange fragmented dreams, memories that faded slowly, leaving their taste-without-meaning behind as tantalizing puzzles.

Joe woke with one thought in his mind, which he expressed aloud immediately. "Multiwave," he said, and let Jailyn give a sigh.

"Must we?" she said.

But she now knew, somehow an inevitability had grown as they slept, up around the idea of investigating those certainties on the multiwave that so enthused Tech First Order Joseph Winslow.

She did not really understand why she knew this; her mind still shrank in a kind of horror from contacting Joe's directly. She did not understand why horror still lurked, but suspected it would continue as long as her mind seethed with the myriad revelations vouchsafed her by the soma. Her nerves felt like teased hair.

"Must we?" Joe repeated aloud. "I . . . I don't know. I seem to have . . . forgotten. But that means I . . . I won't be able to . . . to . . ." And he ran out of words.

Unexpectedly Jailyn found herself offering encouragement. "You'll remember, if it was there and real. And I suppose you could also take some of that soma along."

"He won't let us use it again for a while, you know; he already mentioned that. And I'm sure he wouldn't let us use it when we were alone. Since I now feel strongly we're going to have to leave soon, well . . ."

"Archer?"

"I don't know. One man doesn't bother me . . . Kinsolving's one man, too, of course, but with as many men behind him as several billion solits can buy. Richer than you."

"Richer than my whole family put together," Jailyn said, then smiled Tylerface, finding sudden pleasure in the feel of the muscles as they tensed and relaxed. "I never did stand to come in for more than twenty-odd million—though I did get two million when I turned eighteen."

She giggled, and Joe wanted to wince. "Why can't we talk mind-to-mind? I'm sure we sound like a rare idiot talking to ourselves."

Jailyn was serious again. "Not just this moment, Joe, please. I'm awfully on edge."

"Two million at eighteen," Joe said, shrugging and reverting to the main conversation. "That's salt in the wounds! Too bad it's gone. With money like that, even against a billionaire we might have had a chance, except—uh!"

Jailyn had suddenly tried to take over the Tylerbody —tried to shriek aloud, in fact; and Joe grunted involuntarily with the mixed impulses in Tyler throat.

She had control now, and was laughing wildly for a moment. "Sorry, Joe," she said, gasping for air, "but I remembered. I *remembered!* I'd been so pleased, so full of ideas on what to do with all that money—and the family had their ideas, of course. Well, I hid some of it! I don't know if there's any great amount left— I took a lot back out a couple years later. But I haven't been there since, and—"

Warily Joe took over the voice. "Can you get at it now? How much is there? And where is it?"

"It wasn't much really. There might be 50,000. And to think I used to wonder if I'd been foolish! But, Joe, that's not the point—there's a spare key there too!"

"Key to what?"

"To my spaceship, of course—the *Zipper!* I got it for my eighteenth birthday, along with the money—the flyer must have cost, oh, 200,000 at least."

She paused, then Tylervoice became mournful. "Well, it *was* my spaceship. But later, after Jimmy Tungo and the *Miles High* and all, you know, I gave it away, to old Stanley Thomas. Oh, he wasn't so old, I guess, maybe fifty, but he'd been with the family for years and years, since before I was born. He always treated me like . . . like a person, not a princess. So I gave him the *Zipper*. Gee, that was five years go. I . . . I guess I lost track of Stanley. I don't know whether he's still got it, or even if he's still alive."

"Kimmel's Yaletron outlet—key it into census information, huh? Find him in a jiffy."

"No, not census," she mused. "You're not computer-oriented, that's obvious. Locked Information, Joe. Need-to-know. Very much so. Census information's too risky for general . . ."

"Ok, ok," Joe interposed as Jailyn trailed off into reverie again. "Where are all these goodies tucked away? We can track down the ship somehow."

"Safe-deposit," Jailyn said abstractedly. "Quite safe."

"Oh, Christ! With all your accounts frozen already, you're going to tell me—"

"Poo. I didn't take it out in *my* name, silly! I was all filled with dreams of youth and, well, and two million solits. I used a fake name and used only the mails."

"Great—and what did you use for a return address?"

"Poo again. I rented a hotel room for six months and used that address. Nobody knew; the hotel thought I was Mrs Timothy Finnegan, Mr Finnegan being the account-name. And I made up a signature, and . . . uh-oh," she added in a small voice.

"Signature," said Joe. "Great. With a new set of hands you should be able to do one about as genuine as a plastic diamond."

"No, no," Jailyn responded, brightening. "I used code words, too—I was just a kid, after all. Told them the code words were more important than the signature. Dark hints, and all. I wanted to be on the safe side, just in case I couldn't do the signature just right."

"Mmmm. Well, then, if you write, give the codes and signature . . . can we carry it off?"

Jailyn slumped, overwhelmed once more with a sense of futility. "I don't know; maybe. But wouldn't you say it's worth a try? Fifty thousand and a controls key?"

"Depends on what we're going to use it for, even if we can get it. What *do* we use it for?"

"Well, I suppose—" once more she giggled "—I suppose it's better than sitting around talking to ourselves!"

"I can see it's my cue. I'm supposed to say something like, 'Hey! Let's take the flier and go off to Monstro and Do Something Important with the multi-wave!' Sure."

"I'd *like* to, of course, but if we've got trouble now, that'd only make things worse. I can tell you that un-authorized landing on a multiwave installation would probably land us someplace a little bit worse than New Bellevue . . ."

"But we can't stay here. Do you think Kinsolving and Dr Brian are going to give up on us? Kimmel has a lot of confidence in his security here, whatever it is, but we've *met* those two."

"With 50,000 maybe we could buy off that Archer fellow, and—"

"Outpay Kinsolving? I won't even bother pointing out what's wrong with that picture. And would Kin-solving be fool enough to throw money away on some-one who could be bribed?"

After Jailyn spoke, there was silence for a time as each followed separate lines of thought.

"The thing is," Joe mused aloud after a time, "*seeing* those multiwave generators like that, I realized that it's the harmonics that . . . when we tune the generators we always try to eliminate the harmonics. Hit a note and clean it up. But the sun doesn't emit a 'clean' note! If a generator could be dropped into complete synch with a great-enough mass, it might propel . . ." Joe dropped into subvocalizing, then fell silently into thought.

"Honestly," Jailyn said, "that didn't make any sense to me at all."

There was no response from Joe; Jailyn wrinkled Tylerbrow and shut Tylereyes, and, reluctantly, let her mind slip into resonance with Joe's.

He wasn't holding a strong mental block—but it made little difference. It was the first time she had observed his "professional" mind at work, as she put it to herself; and it made no difference that she was reading his mind in effect. She didn't understand multiwave mechanics, nor its specialized mathematics that Joe was absorbedly manipulating.

Opening Tylereyes, she sighed deeply. "I wish we'd tried thinking at that Yaletron instead," she said aloud, knowing Joe would pay no attention; he had retreated completely into his problems.

"And," she added equitably, "I suppose you'll just let me droop along out here running the body till you're interested in coming back and taking another look at things. . . ."

She attempted to stand up, and fell back dizzily onto the bed—aware as she fell that Joe had taken one quick glimpse and had withdrawn once more, assured they were not going to be hurt by the fall.

"Whew!" Jailyn said softly. "Dizzy—from hunger? I guess. Hm. Trundle down for food if they'll feed me at this hour—whatever it is! Wow! Do I feel crummy. . . ."

Carefully she got up once more, and walked haltingly

to the door. As she opened it she saw Prez coming down the hall.

"Hi!" he called cheerfully. "Thought you might be up. Came to help—had the feeling you might be a little woozy."

As he spoke he came up and caught Tylerbody just as Jailyn started graying out and buckling at the knees.

"Yep, thought so," Prez said calmly. "Come on, all you need is some food. Soma takes the strength out of you sometimes, when you really get deep with it."

Jailyn smiled, weakly. "Thank you. Nice to know there are still a few gentlemen around willing to help a lady in distress!"

She giggled, as Prez did a double take and then laughed sheepishly.

Inside her a single flash, a despairing wail: *I like him! Why couldn't I have met him* before—and she chopped the thought off, tried not to think of it. It was difficult to bear the thought of Tylerbody making love to a woman; the image of it making love to a man was too much for her.

"Archer's still puttering around," Prez said, "though what he expects to learn about the care and feeding of multiminds, *I* don't know. I'd say the man is a fool, if he'd not gotten as far as he has. A fool is the first thing he is not. Not after this morning, I don't call him a fool."

"Are you worried?" she asked as Prez assisted Tylerbody downstairs into the great dining room, which was empty as they arrived.

"Worried? No. Yes. Hm, concerned, say. Even Kimmel is a little concerned by now, I should think. We have our methods for keeping unwanted visitors from our lands, but . . . Well, I might as well tell you. We tried one on Archer and . . . well . . . he ignored it."

Prez helped Tylerbody into a chair at the table, then went to the kitchen and began bringing food back.

"Cold cuts, fresh bread, butter, honey, cheese, some soup if you'd like that."

"Well?" Jailyn said when he had sat down after ferrying in the last batch of food. He didn't seem to want to return to the subject of Archer.

"Well?" she said again, after a pause long enough to indicate she'd given him his chance, "what did you try doing to him?"

"Uh, Kimmel told you about mindtouch—weak and untrustworthy. That's correct as far as it goes. But we have a couple of esper proficients in the area—they occur maybe one in 500,000, as far as we can tell. Usually all they do is project at an unwanted intruder; project, oh, abject fear, let's say. And unwanted intruder crumples to the ground in a heap; and when he picks himself up again, unwanted intruder proceeds very quickly in any direction *but* here. They seldom come back in range. . . .

"It's not that much of a trick, really. Don't get the wrong idea. Anyone who really knew what we were doing could probably block off the effect long enough to get to the farmhouse, where we'd have to take other measures."

He paused and smiled broadly. "Nothing exotic, just a whiff of happygas and then some friendly words about how he doesn't really like this part of Ohio at all, and then he goes to sleep for two days, and when he wakes up we feed him a good dinner and then he goes away and doesn't come back. Or, conversely, seeing as how you've loosed the floodgates of privy information, we can beef up our espers' natural power with linkages to one or more of the rest of us, depending. *That* usually does the trick; trouble is, we can't keep mindtouch up for more than a few seconds like that. Fortunately, our hapless subjects are very pleased to leave after that.

"But we usually don't have to mess with any really

advanced stuff. It's peaceful out here."

"What did you try on Archer, then?"

"Uh, well . . ." Prez seemed to be blushing. "We figured he was a large man and might have a large man's unwillingness to be led around by other people, so we put both our espers on him. Sent him a good scare. Observer told us he turned pale for a minute; then he lit up a pipe, shut his eyes, and relaxed. And after a few minutes our espers started getting headaches. I think Mr Archer knows a little bit about espers.

"At any rate, after he relaxed he just absorbed the fear radiations and reflected 'em right back at our people." Prez shook his head. "Gave 'em a rare jolt, I'll tell you. I never did think there was much importance in esper powers. A vein of genuine ore, no doubt; but a thin vein, very thin."

There was a knock at the front door; Prez frowned, got up, and went into the living room.

"Oh," Jailyn heard Prez say, in an oddly strangled voice. Tylerbody turned and looked toward the front door in the next room, and she felt Joe's presence again.

Prez stood facing the dining room, his face twisted in agony, one arm twisted around and held firmly in the small of his back.

Behind Prez towered a man. He seemed to be a good six and a half feet tall, and might have weighed three hundred pounds.

Seeing Tylerbody, the man urged Prez back to the dining room.

"Be nice now?" he said to Prez, and Prez grimaced. "Why should I?"

"I'll break your arm if you give me serious trouble, that's one reason," the answer came in conversational tones, "and you might be surprised, but I don't really want to do that. I came to talk and then to leave."

"Let me go and we'll talk," Prez offered.

"Thing is," the large man said equitably, "somebody's likely to come by and realize I don't belong here, or you might call out—which I wouldn't advise your doing. I mean that about your arm, and I only want to talk."

"All right," Prez gasped, "just stop with the arm, ok? I won't try to raise an alarm."

Prez sighed with relief as his arm was released. He sat down beside the Tylerbody, and Jailyn could feel Prez shaking with surprised reaction.

"My name's Archer, which you probably guessed, John Archer. I dunno why, but most people think the private detective's always the bad guy." The large man's tone was still conversational. He pulled out a chair and sat down at the table.

"But they usually take him for a fool, too; that sort of evens things out. Take me, now. I know what country people are about. If you're willing to believe me, I'll even tell you I approve, generally speaking. Not everybody in the city's crazy. Which is why I came. I don't intend bringing trouble here."

Joe shook Tylerhead slowly from side to side. "I can't really accept that. You work for Kinsolving. Kinsolving wants us. That's trouble—or are you giving him his money back and throwing in with us?" He tried for bitter sarcasm but Tylervoice broke with the strain; Joe was upset from having to break away from the smoothly flowing stream of mathematics he'd been following.

"Not exactly," Archer said, "but you're close. When I took this job—which I shouldn't have—Kinsolving didn't level with me. He gave me the name Tyler, and a picture, and some other details. But he didn't bother telling me *you* were the famous multimind. That I didn't find out till Cleveland, and it made me feel a little foolish, which is a thing I don't much care for."

"Anyway, one of those lads you beat up on doubled

back and trailed you to the bus stop, and when I chatted with him he wanted to discuss it, after a while. Then I went round to the old geezer at the stop, smoking some country blend so he'd recognize me as a friend, and he mentioned Mansfield. Well, now, about the time I got into Mansfield, I realized *I* was being followed. A private detective is sort of apt to notice another private detective, which is a thing I'd have expected Kinsolving to know. Richards, the guy is. Ok, but dumb.

'So I puttered around a bit, got an idea where you were, and thought about Richards a while. After a while Richards sort of fell over my foot or something, and while I was sitting on his chest helping him get up, we had a nice chat about Mr Kinsolving."

"This is quite a lecture," Prez said, bitterly. "A falling out among—"

"Don't say thieves, my friend," Archer said gently, his eyes almost closed. "I've got a temper as hasn't been seen in five generations of Archers, and I purely hate to lose it because I end up doing so much damage to things, and people, and I'm a peaceable man."

Prez fell silent, but observed Archer more closely while he went on talking.

"Now, I was hired to locate you," Archer said, "not knowing who you were—I suppose Kinsolving thought I was only a dumb ex-cop who couldn't do anything else for his living, and thought he could get away with something. Anyway, Richards told me he'd been hired to bring you back to Kinsolving—I'd already made it clear to Kinsolving I didn't work at things like that without lots of heavy motivation. So he hired Richards. And, when Richards wakes up in a couple of days—he was carrying some happygas and it somehow accidentally went off—he'll probably try to go ahead with Kinsolving's assignment."

Archer looked at Prez and Tylerbody, then shrugged. "That's all. I found you, I said my piece, and now I'll go."

"Just like that?" Jailyn said, amazed. "What about Kinsolving and Richards? I mean, what you've told us, we're going to be *kid*napped; and yet you're just going to amble away and . . . and . . ." She could find no more words.

Archer smiled lazily. "I'm not giving Kinsolving anything on you, if that's what's upsetting you. He'll get a note of resignation with what's left of the retainer after expenses so far, and that's it." Archer shrugged. "What can he do?"

"To you, maybe nothing. To us . . ." Again Jailyn found no more words.

Archer settled back in his chair. "I always did like giving advice; you've just coaxed me. First off, I'd say get away from here. Richards will be in touch with Kinsolving in, oh, say about forty hours."

"How about holding Richards here so he can't get to Kinsolving?" Joe asked.

Archer caught the voice change; his eyes narrowed and he looked closer at Tylerface. Then he sat back again, nodding his head. "No, that's kidnapping," he said cheerfully.

"I don't understand this and I don't much care to," Joe said bitterly.

"Second," Archer went on, "if you've got some place to go to Kinsolving doesn't know about, well, please don't tell me. I want to level with him. I don't want to say more than that I'm off his case and don't know any more about it than he does. But if you've got a place, I'd suggest going there. Just be damned sure he doesn't know where. And offhand I'd say these people here can get you about anywhere—unseen, or at least unnoticed. But don't tell me."

Archer finally heaved himself up onto his feet with

obvious effort. Prez stood up hastily, looking very uneasy.

Archer looked at him closely. "You're not telling me something. You probably should. Out with it."

"Uh, I'd better walk with you down to the old highway. You, uh, might not make it back otherwise—" Prez grinned wryly "—at least not as quickly as you'd like."

Archer smiled satanically. "You're not a fool, either. Thanks for the warning; I'll take it and the aid. Well, folks, I'll be seeing you—or won't, more'n likely. But that's ok, though I admit I'd sorta like to find out, some day, what it's like living inside somebody else's head. . . ."

"You don't really want to know," Jailyn said, chuckling even while she wondered why.

"You sound cheerful enough," Archer said, raising his eyebrows slightly.

"Oh, we have our ups as well as downs," Joe said, and was going to continue but Prez interrupted.

"It's all right," Prez said, so conversationally it took a moment and more to realize he wasn't talking to Archer but past him, "don't do anything to him, he's a friend."

Looking around at the kitchen, they all saw two rather grim-faced youngsters in their teens, each holding a small happygas canister, long thin nozzles pointed straight at Archer's face.

"You tads ever heard about a warned man holding his breath?" Archer said to them, as conversationally as Prez a moment before. "You get the drop on a man like this again, take him out then. You got antidotes, you can always wake him up if you made a mistake. You don't want to let a stranger *know* you're going to zap him with happygas, 'cause, like I say, too many people are smart enough to hold their breath. Well," and he turned back to Tylerbody and Prez, "I've given my quota of advice and then some, for this month anyway. Now then, I'd be happy to take up your offer of escorting me to the road."

And Archer turned and left with Prez, tagging after him and looking unusually distressed. . . .

CHAPTER SIXTEEN

TYLERBODY STAGGERED and was knocked back from Monstro's master console; after long seconds of low gravity, Tylerbody thumped heavily back onto the metal floor with a "whoosh."

Joe felt Benjy, silent, quivering, cowering; Jailyn would not, could not think through pain that he saw cut across nerve endings—in her mind, her mind, he insisted frantically to himself, trying to keep the pain at bay, pain that blocked every effort to think, disabled Jailyn, Benjy. . . .

And that left Joe.

He saw Jailyn's agony, saw the illusion slowing taking command of her mind, even as he knew it was only some new part of their mind, receiving the full effect of Monstro's multiwave generators.

He'd flicked the beast up to standard broadcast, running through basic procedures just to make sure he still had the touch. It was routine, always had been. He wasn't really even paying that much attention; he'd been idly remembering the taste of the last cherry pie they'd had just before leaving Kimmel's, well over a month ago.

He was almost tasting the cherries as he flicked the switch to "standard." The computer registered his command to raise the multiwave broadcast from standby—4,000 cycles—to standard—20,000 cycles—then obeyed the command.

Jailyn had obviously been thinking of something painful at the moment; Joe hadn't noticed, preoccupied with his memory of cherry pie. When the first blast of standard hit, they were suddenly able to perceive the multiwave directly again, as in the soma experience and the momentary spells.

To Joe it was only a momentary affliction, the temporary conviction that ten million tons of cherry pie had suddenly been inflicted upon him simultaneously. He quickly realized what must have happened, and the illusion went away.

He wanted to laugh—but Tylerbody lay on the deck half-catatonic, rigid with the illusion of pain; Jailyn had convinced Benjy the pain was real even while he could sense it wasn't, and he was helpless in this contradiction.

Joe couldn't get through to stand up, much less to stagger back to the console and turn off the generator.

Finally he managed to hunch one shoulder, then get to his knees, get some more muscles under control and lunge toward the console, an awkward low-gravity stagger with complications. It got him close enough to reach up and slap the "revert" pressureplate, lowest on the panel.

Tylerbody sagged back limply in relief and lay staring up at the ceiling, as the multiwave dropped back to standby.

It was long moments before Tylerhead turned and they looked directly at the pseudogravitic centerspace that was the core, the origin of the artificial pulsations, saw them glowing and pulsing in the origin, shimmering and changing and ever-expanding, saw them through fifty meters of metal and rock.

For . . . for God's sake, Joe, what happened?

Never mind that—we can see the multiwave again! We can see it! It was right to come here, and the hell with Transfed; we can make a break-through. I don't know what it's going to be, but if I don't try now I'll never have another chance.

Then let's get started.

They couldn't have said when, precisely, they realized Monstro was the only place left for them to go. And in one sense they knew even that wasn't true, for they could go to Earth easily enough.

But the price for that would have been anonymity—and stagnation. They had to *do* something; they were not ready for the contemplative life, for fields of wheat, for soma, for . . . peace. For now, it tasted too much of their room in New Bellevue.

Kimmel seemed certain they had to do something, if only to break out of the patterns, as he put it. Had Kimmel been a little shaken by Archer? Probably not, was Jailyn's opinion; Joe wasn't so sure.

And it became time to leave, and then they were gone. It took almost a week to get to California; Jailyn's disguised account was in Palo Alto.

Kimmel sent them in a fancar belonging to the farm, and thus they began a series of state-long journeys with a succession of close-mouthed country people.

Joe was starting to gnaw into the problem of the multiwave and its occasional visibility far enough not to care about a lack of conversation; Jailyn was irritated by the silence of their temporary hosts, until she decided they not only didn't care to talk, they didn't even care that they didn't care.

The asteroid's got its own first-level ion drive, Joe thought at Jailyn suddenly, and the Tylerbody jerked.

Great, she said. *We could take it with us to Miami.*

No, no, he answered impatiently. We could evade pursuers long enough . . . well, more than that. I mean it might be possible to tie the ion drive in with the multiwave.

I thought you'd already decided that's what you'd like to do with your new toy, she thought at him; but the sarcasm was muted. She could already see the answer shaping up in his mind.

Before, I only wanted to be able to make the hookup. Now I think I can really do it.

That leaves only the question of what good it'll do to hook them up.

Nobody's ever bothered trying to make the multiwave into a drive, since the early days anyway. It doesn't *push;* all that power just goes into the centerspace, and then . . . presto, the origin of the multiwave. But they can't get it to do anything or go anyplace; it just sits and radiates pseudogravitic thingies that shouldn't even exist. So we've been trying to work out ways to modulate the damn thing so we can at least make it a carrier. Some of the installations—not the ones in the necklace orbit—are trying to pick up possible multiwave broadcasts from other cultures. So far, nothing; but we know we've got a lot to learn about the thing, so nobody's ever worried so far!

It really is like a game for you, isn't it? she asked, feeling warm from the glow of happy contentment coming from Joe as he teased over his favorite topic in his mind.

Well . . . like a toy. And we're looking to see if we can find a game for it.

You're really making me miss my computers! Why don't you let me help you out a little?

Come on in!

And they found themselves opening their minds to each other to their farthest reaches—farther even than the soma had taken them, and in more directions simultaneously, and they both shied back from the awesome empty limits that had suddenly, challengingly, and more than a little frighteningly shown themselves;

and they agreed wordlessly not to look out in those directions again for a while, and went to work on the multiwave. . . .

Their last driver left them within a day's walk of Palo Alto, and, surprisingly, they found they were not far from public transportation.

Once in Palo Alto and a hotel room, they sent a letter to the bank. It carefully cited the rather childish code words; and they received an immediate and favorable reply. That had been that. Jailyn had paid a twenty-year flat fee on the box rental, caught in her youthful flair for drama. Obtaining a refund on the remaining time, over half, would help them track down the space flyer.

That was more difficult. Old Stanley Thomas had died, and a young, unsentimental, and unambitious cousin had sold the *Zipper*.

Joe began to wish they'd been able to hire Archer to help them, but Jailyn had remained serene, and it was only the next day they tracked the *Zipper* to a small rental fleet. Now called the *Kirk*, it was due back from a Venusatellite run in only three days. Its secondary-level ion-beam fields, for planetary landing, made it and similar craft profitable for ferry-fleet operators; taking one ship instead of three was popular with the rich and the time-conscious.

Kimmel had provided them with high-quality, but extremely phony, pilot's I.D.; and they left most of their cash in the fleet owner's office for surety and payment covering an equally phony flight plan for the Venusatellite.

The core mechanisms of the drive banks had not been changed; once off-planet, they used the magnicode key from Jailyn's deposit box to open them and change the flightplan from Venusatellite to Monstro.

A few weeks later they arrived at Monstro, dosed the technician on duty there to keep him quiet, and sent him away in the flyer, with a flight-plan tape end-

ing in a Mars parking orbit. The technician would wake
up in a couple of days, none the worse, with a tape in
the core mechanisms he couldn't get at.

Then they'd set to work, and presently Joe had
flicked the "standard" switch; and now Tylerbody was
slowly getting up off the floor.

Increments, Joe thought. I'll run the thing up
slowly by increments, and set the monitor for vocal
commands. That way we won't be at its mercy.

This time they perceived only a kind of cold hot
brightness, over there through the other side of fifty
feet of reasonably dense materials; the brightness grew
brighter and brighter, though never unbearably.

After a time Joe, checking his monitors, realized they
were at 23,000 cycles. He started to bring this to Jailyn's
attention, but she only shot back a sharp *Hush, now;
concentrate. This is important.*

Then he realized that he had the faint taste of
cherry pie roaming through parts of his mind; and
that Jailyn was fencing with the shadows of great
pain. . . .

He closed Tylereyes and tried to relax, merge his
mind with hers, risking apocalyptic moments. There
was a taste of THEYness now, as he synchronized
with the surface of her thoughts without trying to
probe deeper.

Even coasting on the surface of her mind, he felt
he could see deeper into its pellucid depths now than
ever he had dared before.

And then he was within her mind and part of it before either realized; and it was all right; her mind no
longer sensed the multiwave as pain, though hints of
cherry pie still lurked in backgrounds and corners; and
they lived together waiting while the multiwave grew
stronger and stronger, coldly brighter and brighter in
their minds until its point of origin seemed grown far
beyond the limits of the centerspace at the generator
core; until the core was a part of all the asteroid, and

of the computer, and of Joe's mind and Jailyn's and Benjy's, and Joe tried to say "Enough" to the computer monitor and his voice broke—but the computer dropped the generator back to standby.

Though they were now seated, Tylerbody sagged like wet cloth.

How . . . how much more can it generate? Jailyn asked weakly, at last.

The pressure was rough, yes, I know. I think we got it to about half maximum, let me talk it over with the computer.

We could kill ourselves on this thing, she mused as Joe tapped out symbolic questions.

Ho, ho that we could; but we're not going to. Dammit, come in with me on this; I did a lousy query program again. You're the expert.

Jailyn giggled aloud. *I thought you'd never ask! Come on, last one in . . . ! You know, we're going to have to go into the core area sooner or later, to do this right. We ought to work as closely as possible till then. I can see how you used to hate those "Birth Canal" trips!*

Please! Don't remind me. Here, this query program . . .

And Benjy began whistling "Guantanamero," while the other two concentrated. . . .

Has anyone ever done it? Jailyn asked.

Done what? Joe responded warily.

Actually stuck their head into that focal point there? With the generator on, I mean?

Joe sighed aloud, and nodded.

I don't remember any specific names, though I'll write up the query. He flicked the lightpen over the portable monitor, and the answer came back immediately.

"Three cases on record," read the printout. "Each involved accidental fall through origin point while generator was on full power. Postmortems established probable cause as multiwave damage. Hypothesis (in view of lack of noticeable tissue damage): death was due to psychological factors of indeterminate nature, induced by high-intensity multiwaves."

Hm, that's a bit ominous.

That's full power, remember. Look, we took full power with ease, outside, and look where we are now— right beside it, and it's on standby. Doesn't bother us a bit.

All right, all right. I was going through with it anyway, you know that.

BENJY LIKE FUNNY FEELINGS. MORE NOW?

Well, now, that makes it a two-thirds vote for now. Shall we proceed?

Benjy doesn't have a vote in matters like this— he doesn't have the judgment for it.

BENJY KNOWS SAME THINGS YOU KNOW. BENJY NOT *think* SAME BUT BENJY *know* SAME. BENJY THINK OTHER THINGS YOU NEVER LISTEN TO.

I never heard you give a leading remark before, Benjy—what don't I listen to?

YOU THINK WHEN WE THINK TOGETHER AFTER NICE DRINK FROM NICE KIMMEL YOU SEE STARS AND PLANETS AND THINGS MOVING AROUND YOU NEVER SAW BEFORE. BENJY WAS THE ONE WHO SAW. BENJY SAW HEAVY AND LIGHT, IN AND OUT, LOUD AND SOFT, UP DOWN INSIDE TWIST OUT. NOT UNDERSTAND, BUT SEE. SO YOU SEE THEN. BENJY DOESN'T UNDERSTAND BUT BENJY KNOWS. YOU GO AHEAD. MAKE HEAVY AND GO.

Joe began writing instructions on his portable readout plate. I refuse to believe what I just heard—but I'm not going to argue with it!

I don't blame you, Jailyn added weakly. Benjy's almost wordless thoughts had been accompanied by a moment of sheer total vision, brought back from the peak of their experience so many weeks ago.

Ok, I've got it ready to start us on one cycle. It won't go higher till we're ready.

Without even taking a deep breath Tylerbody leaned forward into the focal origin point.

TICKLES, Benjy's mind giggled.

Does, at that, Joe admitted.

I've got the funny feeling I'm part of the multiwave now, part of the generator, part of the planetoid. But not—

WE ARE, Benjymind said. EVERYTHING IS.

Benjy, you're a born seer; but this doesn't get us much further.

Joe, I can sense the generator directly . . . pseudo-mass functions . . . interaction with subgravitic propagation and interstitial inertia of the plasmoid forces—

Joe moved Tylerhead out of the origin point. "Enough of that for a moment," he said aloud.

AWWWWW, said Benjymind. THAT WAS FUN. FALLING EVERYWHERE, ANYWHERE. GO ANYWHERE.

Maybe, maybe. But let's take this step by step.

Let's get back to it. Are you willing to step up the cycles?

One at a time, first; then, well, we'll see . . .

Joe gave orders to the readout plate with his light pen, then Tylerbody leaned forward into the origin point.

A knifelike opening-up sliced through them, as, at two-second intervals, the multiwave generator rose from 1 cycle to 2, to 3, to 4, to 5, to 6, to 7. At 8 Joe convulsively slapped the "revert" button on the readout and jerked Tylerhead away.

I don't know about you, he thought, his mind in a turmoil, but I just had the conviction that I could modulate the 2-, 4-, 6-, and 8-cycle waves directly. It seems hard to believe, but then, it's not as if we were trying to modify the damn thing in the generator itself. That's where they've all been going wrong—trying to modify the effect before it actually formed in the origin point. All that energy focused in one spot . . .

Does your computer have a brain-wave monitor? Jailyn felt Joe's assent. *If you step up the rate of cyclic increase, key it in for cutoff.*

I don't know; it might think our brainwaves are abnormal already, and what good would that do?

Here, let me do it. They never taught you much about creative programing, that's obvious.

Presently she had instructed the computer to cut off the progression if their EEG changed more than 25 percent in intensity or became erratic past that percentage of their present state. Once more they leaned forward, into the origin point.

8, 10, 20, 30, 60, 80, 100, 200, 250, 300, 350, 700, 800, 900, 1,000 cycles. Joe slapped the "revert."

How's *that* for kicks? he asked with great satisfaction. Here we are a fourth of the way to standby and it hasn't hurt a bit!

I still felt in control of it, even at 1,000, Jailyn remarked. *Sort of, I don't know, sort of as if . . . as if, if I had a generator built into me I could simply ride along the waves, like a . . . a surfboarder, or something.*

It's got to work something like that, Joe responded abstractedly.

Unexpectedly Jailyn broke out into peals of laughter, which fell away into almost echoless silence in the small chamber. *I suppose the first man to think of inventing the wheel was scared of the idea!*

I dunno, but the guy who invented fire probably got his fingers and things burned quite a few times before he realized he hadn't invented it—just come across it.

I'll bet you're trying to warn me to be careful. She felt warmly suffused with happiness, though she could not decide why.

Uh-huh. He dropped back into an abstracted mood for a moment. Shall we try a flash of standby? I'll just flick it on and then drop my hand right onto the "revert"—just for a taste of it.

Jailyn assented and 4,000 cycles of pseudogravitic pulsations throbbed soundlessly through THEIR head and THEY caught Joe before he slapped the "revert" and instead THEY bathed now in the standby and felt the power flow through THEM; and THEY wondered whether THEY could take standard and the propagation increased in a single jump to 20,000 cycles and THEY were blinded with the roar of space and time of blackness stars eternity spreading before between behind above beneath and THEY called for 100,000 cycles and felt the twisting grip of the sun as *its* mass propagated nonpseudogravitic wave functions past the multiwave asteroid and THEY called for 20,000 cycles and found THEMself thrown suddenly against the walls of the chamber, and the generator dropped to standby.

There was silence, save for slow breathing.

BENJY TIRED. WE SLEEP NOW. TOMORROW GO SEE THINGS. SLEEP NOW. SLE

CHAPTER SEVENTEEN

Pardon my malicious glee, but I'm glad you told them to make a careful approach.

Well, Joe's thoughts were cast in gloom, they're still going to be here in 3.7 days.

Do you think there's any likelihood we might hit the wrong harmonic and blow up every craft within our omega range?

Not really, but *they* don't know that. Come on, let's get back to it.

They had slept, and risen to a communications alarm; an Interfed ship had sent them a warning of approach.

Ok, that's done, Joe thought, after several hours of ferrying tie-in lines through the access tunnel. Let's get back to the real work.

At 200,000 cycles, this time THEY withstood the shock of power which had sent THEM reeling the last time THEY had tried. Now THEY were overpoweringly aware—both of the immense forces being propagated, and of the sheer immensity of space, seen directly, perceived directly, gravitic waves rather than light.

THEY perceived the generator's actual mass and its propagation mass. THEY perceived Monstro's mass; THEY perceived the sun's mass; THEY perceived, more dimly, the mass of the entire galaxy, its stars, and the vast energies surging among them.

THEY observed raptly for a timeless time of wonder and Joe slapped the "revert" at last, and THEY continued to perceive in gravitic waves though the generator had once more dropped to standby

and Jailyn broke away from THEM and came back immediately, like a released rubber band flexed for the exercise—if a rubber band needed exercise.

Let's snap down out of it, Jailyn, Joe suggested.

I agree. Jailyn's thought was shaky, wobbly, not in focus.

I sure wish there was a comfortable way to lie down in this damn cage. He looked about the tiny chamber, and felt the sweat running down Tylerback.

"*Joe!*" Jailyn exclaimed aloud. "I just realized— *we've got the answer!*"

Why . . . I believe you're right, he thought back, musing. That last bit—yes, of course! Modulate the origin point directly, sharpen the harmonics to match the sun's natural harmonics . . . the ion-drive tie-in . . . you were right, we'll be like a self-propelled surfboard. With the generator and the ion drive working together, in phase with the sun's mass, we may get to see some very interesting sights. . . .

It . . . it almost sounds too easy.

If you call this easy, what we've been through, well, I don't want to go through anything difficult. Wouldn't I rather be Joe Winslow instead of being trapped in alien flesh and bone? Why, you and I, we might have met, have made love, have fallen in love, felt the spring breezes together, smelled autumn leaves burning. . . . Easy?

Jailyn was silent a moment. *It . . . it isn't easy to think about what might have been, Joe. If our minds . . . had touched . . . before it happened . . . would*

we *have recognized anything in each other? I don't
think so—yet here we are, with common pain and suf-
fering, and you remind me and remind me. No, for us
it isn't easy.*

Come on, let's get back to the main console. I
know we can make a good try at it now—the only
question is whether we can get a jury-rig together
in time that will work. They're going to be here
quick enough, breathing hotly down our neck. Come
on.

The master readout flashed: "Estimated time for
restructuring ion drive into omega-range harmonics:
seven hours."

Well, Joe thought, pushing the chair gently back
from the console, now we take the nice brand-new
plans and we take out the trusty welding torch and
we go and we do it. Hoo, boy. Nothing to it.

It was intricate and demanding work, and it took
fifteen hours instead of seven, and even then they
weren't sure it was right. But a test run of the circuits
got this response on the master readout: "Omega-range
harmonics restructed into basic propulsion unit."

"I suppose I have to believe all this," Jailyn said
aloud, and Tylervoice was raspy with the body's weariness. "Should we get on with the last act now, or get
some sleep first?"

They tried to nap, and could not; and went to the
generator chamber. The computer's got files on several million stars, and it's got a pretty good tracking
system. All I need is to augment the program a
little and it should be able to let us know where we
are no matter where we end up . . . as long as
we're alive in one piece and somewhere in this
galaxy. Then an automatic cutoff set, say, half a
second after the star patterns shift, if they do, and
we'll be safe from that end.

The programs were entered, and Joe ignited the first-level ion drive. Slowly Monstro began to move out of its orbit, Monstro's angle being intended to carry them perpendicular to the orbital plane.

Tylerbody breathed deeply a number of times; then Joe flicked on the multiwave generator, running the cycles quickly up to 250,000, while Tylerhead once more was shoved forward into the origin point of the multi-wave.

Then THEY found THEMSELF once more bathed in the multiwave, like dust motes dancing in sunshine-filled air, and THEY effortlessly worked and reworked the multiwave directly with THEIR mind until THEY paused, with the multiwave in full resonance with the sun's natural gravitic radiation.

Joe dropped down for a last look round, uselessly, then THEY were back.

THEY no longer were thinking in discrete blocks of information; instead THEY flowed with the flow of power THEY delicately manipulated, aware of the almost inconceivable mass of the sun, far more powerful than Monstro's greatest potential pseudogravitic function. And *that* was powered by hydrofusion capable of melting all the ice on Greenland in forty-eight hours —if the power could be dispersed efficiently over such a vast area.

THEY hovered within the now-familiar radiation; it was ultimate nonverbal experience. Later, even much later, THEY refused to bother even to try to put it into words, other than to indicate the general area of the sequence of events.

Then THEY took one last deep breath and engaged the ion drive—and on the aft plate the sun shrank rapidly to a distant point while half a second later the ion drive shut off automatically.

YET in that brief moment it was to THEM as if THEY were free for the first time since the match of time had begun burning; not Monstro but THEY sped at thought's speed past the silent suns through the silent endlessnesses; and to THEM THEY were dancing together as three pure beings of twined energy from sun and ion drive and multiwave generator; and THEY soared through vastness after vastness and caught hold of suns in their flight and harmonized with them and used them to push THEM on faster and faster in their flickering through the dark- and light-spangled infinities; and then the energies were draining away, dying down as THEY flashed from sun to sun till THEY could no longer move the ship and they were motionless again among the tapestried richness of space and stars keeping endless company in poised blind watchfulness. . . .

Jailyn fell away from THEIR mind and Joe followed her down away from THEMSELF and stayed with her in comforting silence while she wrestled with her mind that wanted to scream with the lost horror of the endless panorama of meaningless patternless dotted spatters of light, gold cold blue steady light. . . .

And then Tylerbody was shaking and laughing and sobbing all at once with relief and joy, and THEY hugged THEMSELF and brought the generator back up to full power and THEY reached out and caught a star in the power of THEIR augmented mind and with it threw the ship again and then again, darting about among the great canyons of stars and clouds of gas and sleets of energies from all directions, until Jailyn dropped down once more. . . .

"Joe," Tylervoice croaked hoarsely, "I . . . I'm chilled down deep inside muscle and bone and heart, and happy too, but . . . let's go home . . . if we can. . . ." She rested there some moments; then rejoined Joe.

THEY spoke to the computer and learned the direction of THEIR own so-ordinary star, and THEY reached out and flung THEMSELF among the silent

radiances, and there was the sun, and THEY reached
for it and brought THEMSELF closer, closer, and
Earth was there and THEY reached for it too and
brought THEMSELF closer till THEY had to stop

—two million miles from the twin planets, the Earth
and moon, and the intercom alarm clashed almost immediately, and THEY opened vocal circuits in radio
frequencies and pondered what to tell THEIR race
about the stars that were now within THEIR reach,
and then THEY knew that the secret could be
told only to another Starmind—the name was there
almost without THEIR bidding, and Joe dropped
away.

One, they can't catch us. Two, we can ship anyone we wish to, anywhere, we want to agree to take
him. Three, therefore we hold all the cards.

*All we need to do is to find out what game we want
to play. . . .*

Well, did *you* sense any other multiwave ships
out there?

Of course not. We're the first—

The first from Earth. What about the other intelligent races we know must be out there?

*Do you know, if there'd been any multiwave activity
in all that immense volume of space we zipped through,
I think we'd have noticed it.*

So there may or may not be life out there, but
they probably don't have the multiwave—at least
not within the nearest . . . let's check the computer. Yes. Within the nearest 3,000-odd light-years.
I think that will do for openers.

I wonder when the reaction hits us.

Soon enough; come on, we've got work to do.

Joe cleared his throat and blew gently at the intercom mike, while he chose the first few words that would
begin to let mankind know what was about to happen
to it. If there were no life forms with f-t-l capabilities

within 3,000 light-years, that gave men a fair-sized bit of volume to play around with. . . .

Then he began to speak on Earth hailing frequencies, overriding their noisy protests and questions.

"Hm. Ah, you're not going to believe this, but . . ."

AFTERWARD . . .

(FROM CLOSONJON'S *Early Annals*):

With the multiwave drive under their sole control, the Starmind might simply have reacted to stress by asserting a stressed will to power, might have used the drive to lever Transfed into any position of subordinance the Starmind might have chosen.

It took time to work out the terms; they were benign. The Starmind insisted successfully on a Starmind Guild —to which impossible hundreds of thousands initially applied, most later to drop away before the finality of the inherently necessary double-transplant.

It was of course the transplanting of two minds into contact with a third that produced the breadth of mind required to perceive and manipulate the multiwave directly; and thus too it is that no life form so far discovered has had the fortune to produce a sufficiently similar effect.

The Guild rapidly produced other Starminds, and the race began its hegira out into the universe.

After the formation of the Starmind Guild, the private affairs of the first Starmind disappeared from any sort of public view, and indeed are dealt with in none of the great libraries of the galaxy.

But man's problems were not solved by the Starmind, nor by the Guild, nor by the expansion to the stars; nor likely will they be solved in the afterdays of the great winds of change which even now whistle soundlessly through the Prime Decants.

Not solved—multiplied, by tens and hundreds and thousands and then at last millions of planets occupied by man under the careful initial supervision of the Guild. For the Guild would not permit man to take or to exploit in any fashion any planet with intelligent life forms (and though men always found ways to bend such restrictions, and on the later farther frontiers to begin to break them with some impunity, these are tales for other days' telling).

The Starmind gave mankind the galaxy—or as much as conscience allowed.

Characteristically for the race, the Starmind could not do this without constant struggle against the very forces they were unwittingly trying to aid—and did aid. And it was not that the Starmind at last failed to perceive this; for in a characteristic gesture of their own, they enlisted (as one of their major supporters and later bulwarks in establishing the Guild beyond question), none other than that driven Kinsolving who so desperately sought the glimmering vision of personal immortality. Truthfully they told him he might yet find his answer—among the infinite voids and masses and distances of space, where only the Guild could take him; and he joined them; and the die was cast outward and away; and man's fate became one with the galaxy's; and that, indeed, is another story.

Yet some may be dissatisfied, and wonder still if the Starmind found that peace of inner mind so desperately fought for under the impossible conditions imposed on them by fate; and I can only answer thus: that what they found was what they searched for, and the search was what they found; they had to grow to find they *had* to grow, and for all we know their Merry Quest continues to this day; which is yet another story, and not yet told.

—Closonjon's *Early Annals*,
Vinavex IV, Torbendus,
Decant Seventh Prime,
published for the
thousandth anniversary
of the Starmind

In Science Fiction
Ballantine Books Brings You
the Best of the Established Authors
and the Most Exciting New Writers